Luke closed the inches between them and laid his lips on Mel's, igniting sparks, heat, the quick flare of lust, the slower burn of something remembered, something deeper.

A few stunned seconds passed, then her mouth went pliant beneath his. He felt the faint shiver run through her body and his own jerked in response. Oh, yeah, they still had it. That same recognition, that same magnetic attraction that had drawn him across the crowded function center the instant he'd laid eyes on her at his father's cocktail party.

Then he felt her hand against his chest, heard the muffled sound in her throat. His primitive instincts howled in protest as he pulled back to search her eyes. Enough time to see the light of passion fade to that wariness again.

"I'm different now, Luke. We both are."

"You never know—that might work for us. It was working fine a moment ago."

For another moment she met his gaze, with an honest and open longing that echoed deep in his gut, then as if she'd flicked a switch her expression changed.

Unseen shadows prowled the space that had been humming with promise. She hugged her arms and turned away. "I don't think so."

When not teaching or writing, **ANNE OLIVER** loves nothing more than escaping into a book. She keeps a box of tissues handy—her favorite stories are intense, passionate, against-all-odds romances. Eight years ago, she began creating her own characters in paranormal and time-travel adventures, before turning to contemporary romance. Other interests include quilting, astronomy, all things Scottish and eating anything she doesn't have to cook. Sharing her characters' journeys with readers all over the world is a privilege... and a dream come true. Anne lives in Adelaide, South Australia, and has two adult children. Visit her website at www.anne-oliver.com. She loves to hear from readers. Email her at anne@anne-oliver.com.

Other titles by Anne Oliver available in ebook format:

Harlequin Presents® Extra

THE EX FACTOR
ANNE OLIVER

~ The Ex Files ~

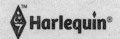

TORONTO NEW YORK LONDON
AMSTERDAM PARIS SYDNEY HAMBURG
STOCKHOLM ATHENS TOKYO MILAN MADRID
PRAGUE WARSAW BUDAPEST AUCKLAND

Recycling programs
for this product may
not exist in your area.

ISBN-13: 978-0-373-52864-6

THE EX FACTOR

First North American Publication 2012

www.Harlequin.com

Printed in U.S.A.

THE EX FACTOR

When I was writing
One Night Before Marriage, Melanie began
demanding her own story. So here it is.

This book is dedicated to my children,
Matthew and Rachel, who told me to
"get a life" when they saw me spending
my weekends at the computer.
Thanks, guys, for putting up with me
all those early years. I love you both.
Thanks to Trish Morey
for her encouragement when things got sticky,
and especially to Meg Sleightholme
for her invaluable advice.

CHAPTER ONE

THE man in her bed had a body built for giving pleasure, chiselled and polished to sinful perfection.

Melanie Sawyer hadn't sinned, perfect or otherwise, in far too long.

So she absorbed the gilded sheen of his skin in the early morning light, traced the wide plane of his back and the long furrow of his spine with hungry eyes. And down, to where the curve of a taut backside disappeared beneath her fluffy pink and tangerine throwover.

It wasn't only her eyes that were hungry. Her lips tingled and her fingers itched to explore the textures of skin and hair. That neat little earlobe, the sharp wedge of shoulder blade. But she only watched, entranced, not moving in case she woke him and spoiled the moment.

He murmured something in his sleep and rubbed his cheek against her pillow, the rasp of stubble sharp against crisp cotton. Her breath caught at the intimacy of his naked flesh sliding over her linen. He faced away from her so she couldn't see his features, but his dark hair was thick and tousled and utterly touchable.

A shame he wasn't awake.

A shame she wasn't in bed with him.

Adam's guy friends had slept over before. But not this particular one. And not in her bed.

With her gaze glued to the delicious sight, she unwound her scarf and set it on her suitcase beside her. Undid the top button of her suddenly too-tight sweater. Was the rest of him naked under that sheet? God, she hoped so. The thought made her blood pump faster, thicker, warming places that hadn't been warmed in a while. A long while. It had been five years since she'd had the pleasure of up close and horizontal.

She was a nurse, she'd seen more than her fair share of naked men, but the fact that this one was snuggled up with her pillow like temptation personified…well, her expectations were high.

Who was this guy anyway?

She glanced over her shoulder at the living-room destruction for any sign of a wallet or ID. Nope. Just a pile of action DVDs amongst greasy take-away containers and beer bottles—the drawback to having a male flatmate, she supposed, although, to be fair to Adam, she had come home from the conference a day earlier than expected.

A low rough-throated rumble from across the room rolled through her senses, drawing her attention back to her bed and its current occupant. With unapologetic interest—and, yeah, anticipation—she leaned against the doorjamb and watched him come to. Watched the sinewy forearms twist as his long fingers bunched and flexed around her pillow. Then he stretched, a lethargic shift and tensing of bone and muscle and golden skin, and rolled onto his back.

Everything inside her froze and fractured.

Luke Delaney.

No! Luke was an engineering geologist in Central Australia somewhere, not here in Sydney.

She saw the same shock register in his too-familiar mocha eyes as they locked gazes and she struggled to draw air. His lazy leonine posture vanished as he pushed up to a sitting position and ran a hand over his eyes as if he, too, was having trouble processing the information.

In that instant subtle changes snapped through her stunned brain. His body had grown firmer and more muscled over the past five years. His hair was shorter. The lines fanning out from his eyes were deeper. But his gorgeous mouth was the same.

Full with a tiny upward tilt at one corner, as if he were about to smile.

But he didn't smile. He swore—a soft short word beneath his breath before he said, 'Melanie.'

His voice reverberated through her bones, deeper, richer than she remembered—and she remembered very well. His velvet whispers in her ear, against her throat, on her breast. The way he murmured her name as he slid inside her.

He scrubbed at his face, then began shifting to the edge of the bed. 'When Adam said "Melanie"... Hell. I'm sorry. I should've grabbed the couch, but Adam said—'

'Stop!' She threw up a hand, hating the desperation she heard in her voice. Was he naked under there? God, she hoped not.

Once she'd have torn back the sheet herself and gloried in his hot, hard masculinity. Her horrified gaze shot back to his face. A more weathered face, but no less handsome. His complexion was a darker sun-stroked colour, but she felt none of that warm familiarity as he studied her through dark, impassive eyes.

One large bronzed hand curled around the edge of the sheet. 'It's okay, Mel,' he said at last. 'I'm decent.'

That was a matter for debate, she thought as he rose, giving her an eyeful of muscular torso covered only by a pair of black briefs, which did little to hide his impressive morning bulge...

Oh, dear God. She turned away, her face hot as wicked thoughts seared through her brain. At least he was out of her bed. 'When you're ready...' *When you're covered.*

She turned and headed back to the living room, grabbed the coffee plunger with its inch of black sludge and carried it to the kitchen. Some sort of conversation was inevitable and she needed a shot or three of caffeine first.

Where was Adam when she needed a buffer? His car was in the underground park next to hers, his bedroom door was shut. She drew in a breath as she dumped coffee into the plunger and savoured its steadying aroma.

She should've stayed in Canberra. Come home tonight like

everyone else. Perhaps she'd have avoided this now inevitable reunion. The memories reared up and the secret she'd thought she'd buried turned over in her breast and throbbed to life again.

Luke continued to stare at the empty doorway after she'd gone. Melanie. *His* Melanie. Her imprint was still seared onto his eyeballs. Curves and colours—tight yellow sweater, a purple skirt above a tantalising flash of leg, knee-high furry beige boots tied up with laces... So Technicolor, so vibrant. So Mel.

Still the most beguiling woman he'd ever met.

And he'd spent the night in her bed.

His fingers clenched at his sides, tension gripped his gut. One look was all he needed to get the adrenaline pumping, his body tensing in anticipation. He remembered how it had been between them—hot, urgent, a fast-track ride to paradise. He'd always wondered how he'd react if he saw her again. Whether the old desires and needs lived up to the memory.

Now he knew, and the knowledge did nothing to reassure him. He forced his hands to uncurl, fought the impulse to leap up and follow the tempting sway of her hips beneath that skirt, the subtle fragrance of roses and vanilla she'd left drifting in the air.

Living with Adam Trent, for Pete's sake. He sucked in a breath. Adam had told him he shared with a nurse, but *this* nurse? He tried unsuccessfully to reconcile the Melanie he remembered with one in a starched white uniform and crêpe-soled shoes.

Which didn't tell him squat about her personal life, Luke thought, grabbing his jeans from the floor. A glance around her room gave no hint. Only a tiny framed snapshot he'd not noticed on her dressing table last night—Mel and her sister, Carissa.

He studied it a moment. Yeah, still those same sultry lips and dark hair he'd fantasised about too often for his peace of mind. No men, then—at least none that rated a pictorial reminder. Relief pumped through Luke, instantly recognised and denied.

Whoa. He shook his head to clear the residual haze that had surrounded him since he'd woken to find that familiar pair of exotic grey eyes watching him. Her love life was none of his business. Her *life* was none of his business. Not since they'd gone their separate ways.

A glimmer of the emotion that had always accompanied her image spun through him like old gold. Part of him wanted to get the hell out, go home, crawl into bed again—his *own* bed—and put this whole morning into some sort of perspective. Another part wanted to stay, to rework that final scene from five years ago into something different, something that might have lasted.

But she hadn't wanted long-term.

He pulled on yesterday's sweater, and made a quick trip to the adjoining bathroom. The reflection in the mirror as he splashed his face with cold water reminded him he wasn't the guy Mel knew anymore either. What would they make of each other now? The band around his gut tightened and he leaned over the basin to eyeball himself. *You don't want to know.*

But one step into the living room, he came to a halt. She was holding a pot of steaming coffee, her buttercup top a stunning foil for the long sweep of coal-black hair, looking as fresh as an early spring daffodil. Quite simply, she took his breath away.

The colour in her cheeks flared a fragile peach as she met his gaze across the room. He'd seen the four seasons in those eyes and for a heartbeat he thought he saw a glint of summer joy behind the clouded depths before they dulled to a neutral stare.

Those eyes had haunted his dreams.

He couldn't linger because she tore her gaze away and crossed to the coffee-table. Her body still had the same concise curves and long, lean lines, the same tilt to her head that set her hair swinging as she set the coffee and mugs down. If she'd changed physically in any way it was only to radiate that inner beauty women seemed to gain as they matured.

His heart stalled in his chest and he had to swallow to ease the dry knot in his throat.

'Coffee?' Her eyes flicked down as she poured him a mug.

'Thanks.' Something strong and wet at least—

'You still take sugar?'

'Yes.'

As he crossed the room to join her she leaned over to pour her own mug. The seductive curves of her breasts pressed intimately against her sweater as she straightened. Sensation burned in his blood, a punch of heat that left him breathless.

'So…' She lifted her mug, wrapped white-knuckled fingers around it and sank onto a faded brown couch as far away from him as she could get. 'What are you doing here?'

'Catching up with Adam.' Gripping his own cup of the fortifying liquid, he remained standing. 'Adam's an old high-school buddy. We had a few drinks, he offered me a bed, said his flatmate wasn't due back till later today.'

'Oh.'

Was that disappointment or relief he heard in her voice? He told himself it didn't matter. One social coffee, a few moments of civilised conversation and he was out of here. 'I'm sorry if I inconvenienced you.'

She lifted a shoulder. 'I…didn't know you were back in Sydney,' she murmured, then frowned into her mug.

'Because we never kept in contact.' The room fell silent as memories flickered like shadows between them. He shook them away. No trips down memory lane. No questions, no blame. Leaning over to set his spoon on the tray with a decisive clink, he said, 'You came home early, then. A conference, wasn't it?'

She nodded. 'My room-mate was a chronic snorer. I couldn't stand it another minute so at three a.m. I packed up and drove home.'

And not quite straight into his arms. 'Strange how fate works.'

An almost-smile touched her lips. 'You sound like Carissa.'

'And how is she?'

'Happily married and very pregnant.'

'Glad to hear it.' He paused a beat before asking, 'And you?'

Her eyes flashed, a lightning bolt that hit him dead centre. 'Single. And still loving it.'

So why the hard-edged animosity in her voice? As if she was trying to convince herself? He acknowledged the strike with a nod and waited for her to ask about him, swallowed a fleeting disappointment when she didn't.

Instead, she said, 'How are your parents enjoying having you back?'

Her tone had an underlying bitterness to it, a puzzle since she'd only met his father once and his parents had been overseas when they'd dated. 'They don't know yet. Dad's not been well so they've gone to Stradbroke Island for a couple of weeks to soak up some sun. I'm in that big old house on my own.'

He could see it in her eyes—*The house my mother cleaned twice a week*. He had a sudden flashback of the first time he'd met Melanie at her parents' funeral. He'd offered his condolences to both sisters on behalf of his parents who'd elected Luke to represent them, but it had been Melanie who'd caught his interest.

Barely a respectable two months' grieving period later and a few days before his parents had left for Europe he'd finagled it with the catering firm so she worked one of his father's business functions. The Bohemian waitress looking for excitement and new experiences. Oh, yeah, they'd found that all right, but the relationship had ended three months later.

'What made you choose nursing?' He dumped an extra spoonful of sugar into his mug to sweeten the suddenly sour taste in his mouth. 'I'd've thought it would be the last thing you'd choose. You couldn't even stand the sight of blood.'

Or vomit, for that matter. His stomach spasmed at the mere thought of Luna Park's high-rolling ride she'd talked him into. Now those golden days of fun and laughter and love in the summer sun seemed like another lifetime.

Her eyes flicked away as if she couldn't bring herself to meet his gaze. She rose and walked to the window. 'It was something I needed—*need*—to do.'

If he hadn't known better he'd have said she looked fragile. 'What happened?'

'Life happened.' She massaged the heel of her hand over her heart. 'It was time to get serious.'

'Serious?' Mel didn't do serious. He'd realised that on their last night as lovers. His fingers tightened on his mug as the blow-by-blow scene roared to life behind his eyes. He'd been the idiot who'd thought it could be something more.

Melanie flinched at the sarcasm in Luke's voice then made the mistake of turning. He was one dangerous step away, six feet plus of emotionally charged man.

'Yes, serious,' she fired back, her spine stiffening at his scepticism. But she couldn't blame him—she'd been a different person when they'd met. Their relationship had been hot and intense...and temporary. A firecracker destined to die.

A fling.

What else could it be? A waitress and a rich man's son? Never mind that she'd done something with her life since. 'It's in the past, Luke, leave it there.'

'You're happy, then? Life's good?'

'Never been better.' She meant it. She was doing what she loved: helping sick kids. It was enough.

It had to be enough.

At the sound of a door opening they both turned as a bleary-eyed Adam appeared. 'I thought I heard voices,' he said. At least he had the discretion not to mention the tone of those voices. 'I hear you two have...ah...introduced yourselves.'

'Morning, Adam.' Melanie stared at her flatmate. He'd mentioned Luke, but she hadn't realised he'd meant Luke Delaney.

'I was just leaving.' Luke set his still-half-full mug on the table, nodded to Adam. 'It was good to catch up.'

'Stay for breakfast,' Adam said. 'Mel makes the best pancakes and maple syrup this side of the Pacific.'

Drizzled with maple syrup... Her toes curled inside her boots at a particularly erotic memory. Head down, she busied herself tidying the coffee-table.

'I'm sure she does,' Melanie heard Luke say before she could refuse, jangling keys as he fished them from his pocket. 'I've got to run.'

'I think these are yours,' she said, glancing at the DVDs as she picked them up and held them out for him at arm's length. 'I guess it gets lonely…wherever you are.'

His fingers slid against hers as he took them from her with that almost-smile on his lips. Oh, that familiar heat, that slow burn snaked its way through skin and bone to wrap cunningly around her heart's memory.

'You never did ask where that was,' he murmured.

No, but it was already too much that she knew where he'd been last night.

He leaned close so only she could hear, his breath hot against her cheek, eyes smouldering with a lambent heat that burned her from the inside out. 'The sex was great though, wasn't it?'

She gasped inwardly at his words, not mocking but sincere, brutally honest in fact. And gulped as the old familiar ache clenched deep in her belly.

His gaze lingered on her lips a moment and she swore she felt his touch. Then he straightened, waved a casual farewell to Adam. 'See you later.'

Rubbing her arms against the rawness of newly awakened emotions, Mel watched the door close behind him. Until Adam's whistle between his teeth startled the wits out of her.

'Is there an electrical storm in here or what? I could literally see the sparks. Sorry if I overstepped the line with the bed. I didn't think you'd be back so early.' His eyes narrowed and she fought the urge to look away. 'Nor did I expect you to be so…uptight—if that's the right word. You okay?'

Mel poured herself another fortifying coffee. 'I'm fine, and anyway it's too late now, the damage is done.'

'What damage?'

She rolled her eyes heavenward. 'The sheets, Adam.'

'The sheets?' He ran a hand through bed-spiked hair. 'I was going to make sure the bed was tidy so you didn't notice.'

'You didn't think I'd notice a man had slept in my bed?'

'To be honest, no.' A grin tilted the corner of his mouth. 'Luke's okay, Mel.' Adam sprawled out on the sofa and dipped a spoon into last night's Chinese. 'And he's made a fortune overseas.' He pointed his spoon at her. 'Most women would find that a plus.'

Overseas? What about the job in Queensland? she wanted to ask—but, of course, she couldn't. Not without going into the sordid details of their history and she really couldn't face that right now. Easier to pretend she'd never met him. 'Doing... what?' she prompted, keeping her tone casual.

'He's an engineering geologist,' he said between spoonfuls. 'Working alongside civil engineers, designing bridges et cetera et cetera. He's been involved in a huge development in Dubai.' A mischievous glint winked in his blue eyes. 'Ah...that auction you girls are planning...'

Huh? The silent auction where everyone was paired off with a member of the opposite sex for the evening? 'No!' With her luck she'd draw his number. *Oh, no. No way.*

'I can vouch for him, Mel. He's single, no risk and good company. The guy could use some female companionship while he's here. It's for charity and he's got money to burn.'

While he's here? Temporarily, then. Thank God. She shrugged, picked up a DVD cover and pretended to check out the blurb. 'He may look—' *like every woman's fantasy* '—okay, but, from a female perspective, he needs more than just a honed body and a sexy smile.'

But they could have used the money. Unlike the others, her prize didn't include her—it was strictly a BYO partner deal. So why was she so against Adam's idea? Because she didn't want to think of Luke paired off with any of her colleagues. She'd hear about it and even after all this time she didn't know if she could deal with that.

'It's too late,' she said, rubbing her arms with the chill that had suddenly wrapped around her. 'The bids closed yesterday.'

But Adam merely grinned as he stacked the empty containers. She frowned as apprehension shivered over her skin. When Adam grinned that way and didn't offer up some comeback line, it usually meant he knew something she didn't. Anyway you looked at it, it spelled trouble.

CHAPTER TWO

THAT night Melanie couldn't sleep. Probably because she hadn't been able to bring herself to change the sheets. *Stupid.* Even worse, she'd left off her night-shirt and slipped naked into bed.

She breathed in the lingering scent of Luke's hair on her pillow. Luke had slept *here;* his hot skin had rubbed over this very spot. Had he been restless too? Had he tossed and turned, maybe subconsciously remembering her scent?

The sheet's texture abraded the sensitive parts of her body. The suddenly overly sensitive parts of her body. She felt like a ripe peach—one fingertip on the right spot and she'd explode right out of her over-tight skin.

Sighing, she moved to a cooler patch of the bed in an effort to ease the aching fullness and tried to concentrate on the soothing patter of light rain against the window. Luke had always been able to turn her on with just a look.

It took a very good man to make that happen, in her opinion, even if she'd only ever had two other men before him to make a comparison. And Luke had been *very* good at his work. Dear Lord, she huffed, plumping her pillow for the umpteenth time. He'd woken the dormant nymphomaniac in her.

She hadn't been with a man since Luke. She'd come close on more than one occasion—after all, she'd told herself she needed to move on with her life, but in those three short months Luke had changed her. In so many ways.

But then she'd never been involved with anyone like Luke, who was older and more worldly…and rich. What did she know about wealth? Even now she couldn't balance her own cheque book.

He'd wanted her for sex. Hadn't he all but told her that this morning? And she wasn't ashamed to admit she'd been only too willing to oblige. But when it came to anything more serious, he'd made no secret about wanting a family. On the other hand, Melanie felt too young to settle down and wanted so much more than to settle in the suburbs with a couple of kids and play at being a rich man's wife.

Not that he'd have ever asked her. She knew the kind of women Luke preferred for that role. As a functions waitress, she'd seen him with elegant females in formal classic attire before he'd ever noticed her. Well-bred women who'd give him equally well-bred children.

She'd told herself it didn't hurt, it didn't matter, that their lives were never going to mesh, why not just enjoy the ride for as long as it lasted? But it *did* hurt, she'd discovered on that final night.

It had been hot, she remembered, with the window open and the air alive with summer sounds and scents. Luke had rolled off her, leaving her sweat-damp skin cooling in the night air.

He'd blown out a satisfied breath. 'That was—'

'Yes. It was.' She closed her eyes a moment to savour the last time she'd feel his body against hers. 'But now I guess it's over, huh?' Words she'd thought would be easy caught in her throat, which suddenly seemed unbearably tight.

She felt him tense beside her. 'Over? Why?'

'No promises on either side, Luke. Wasn't that what you wanted? Just hot, uncomplicated sex.'

'Uncomplicated?' His voice rasped against her ear. 'You're the most complicated woman I know.' He frowned as he rose from the bed, a bronzed god. An angry god. Angry because she'd found out what he'd conveniently kept from her the whole time they'd been together? 'What's wrong?'

She sat up, dragging the sheet with her. 'I worked a ladies' luncheon today. Apparently your wedding's going to be the social event of the season—'

His eyes glinted with something like menace. 'Care to fill me in on who the bride is?' His voice was controlled but the muscle tick in his rigid jaw told another story.

'That girl, Eleanor with the fancy surname—they had a photo of the two of you together.'

'McDonald-Smythe. Hearsay, Mel.' The bed dipped as he sat down beside her and cupped her elbows. 'Don't you know how the upper class loves to spread gossip and lies?'

'You want to talk about lies?' She tried to shake him off but his grip was relentless. 'Why did they have a picture of the two of you at the Melbourne Cup?'

He closed his eyes briefly. *To remember or think up an excuse?*

'That was November,' he said. 'You and I'd gotten together— what—a week earlier? You knew I flew to Melbourne for the day. I met up with a lot of people, I didn't think you needed a detailed inventory.'

No. But there had been other times in those three short months when he'd gone interstate for job interviews, or off somewhere on business. He'd never asked her to accompany him.

It simply highlighted what had been clear from the outset. 'A waitress isn't in your family's grand plan for you.' She jerked free of his hands and this time he let her go.

He looked away, obviously aware of the truth in her statement but refusing to acknowledge what was expected of him. 'What about my plans?' His face darkened, the veins in his neck stood out like ropes. 'As it happens I've been offered a geological position in central Queensland. And I'm taking it.'

In the beat of angry silence that followed she held her breath. He inhaled, as if to add something, then paused. Why didn't he just say it? she screamed silently. *It's been fun but now it's over.*

She gritted her teeth. That was how it was supposed to have been for both of them. So why did it feel so bad?

'Well, then, that's good timing.' She heard the unnaturally high tone in her voice as she reached for her clothes. She might *think* the bottom had fallen out of her inexperienced little world, but it hadn't—she wouldn't let it. 'I heard there are jobs going up north at a new resort.' She didn't look at him but hardened and cemented her resolve. Better to leave than be left. Deep down she knew she'd never fit into his life. She couldn't compete with the rich women who surrounded him.

'Is that what you want, Mel?' she heard him say behind her.

'It's time to move on,' she said, turning towards him but not looking at him, hiding behind an over-bright smile and careless shrug. 'The thing is, I've realised we're too different to make anything more of what we have. We had some great times but it was never going to be permanent between us, Luke.'

'You really believe that, then?' He shook his head. 'Either I've misjudged you or you're one hell of a liar…'

In her own bed, Melanie shook off the images she'd never been able to erase and stared at her ceiling in the dimness. Five years on, she realised perhaps she'd been the liar after all. She'd left Sydney the next day with a vow never to let a man get to her on that level again.

But now that man was back.

Late the following afternoon, Luke negotiated the Lincoln-green Ferrari he'd hired through Sydney's traffic as if he'd never left. A dream run after some of the overcrowded cities he'd lived in.

Which gave him time to think about his father's phone call that morning.

He flipped his indicator and changed lanes. Scowled. When Dad had mentioned 'getting down to business' he hadn't meant the string of restaurants he'd turned into a series of successful franchises over the years. He'd meant the business of Luke getting married and giving him a grandson.

Still, Dad had finally accepted the fact that Luke had made his own wealth and didn't want to inherit his fortune. Now he wanted to force it onto some poor kid who wasn't even born yet.

Dad was a stubborn man, and Mum—he shook his head— she went along with whatever Dad decided. As much as he loved her, he didn't think he could stand such a docile wife.

Which of course segued straight to Melanie—the antithesis of docile. She'd have given him more of an adventure than a marriage. What would his parents have made of her? he wondered, a wry grin tilting the corner of his mouth. The way she dressed, her take on upper-crust society and its conventions.

She'd lured him into having sex in the ornamental fountain on the front lawn one hot night. His grin softened at the memory. He'd never looked at the water feature in quite the same way again, and poor Mum; she'd never got to the bottom of what—or who—had messed with her water lilies.

Damn. He slammed a hand on the steering wheel and hit the accelerator, overtook a Porsche, slowed to an immediate crawl at the next intersection. Five years ago and the memory still made him hard. At least Adam's suggestion that they go for drinks might take the heat out of his frustration.

Seeing Melanie again had brought the past back. With his degree fresh under his belt, Luke had accepted his first job in the outback at age twenty-two. Five years ago he'd been back in Sydney on the lookout for something more challenging than the eight years he'd put into a Western Australian mining operation. Then he'd met Melanie.

He'd done the unthinkable and fallen for her—so different from the women he'd always been attracted to—and when he'd won the position in Queensland he'd intended asking her to take a chance and go with him. But she'd had her own plans, on a different road—plans that didn't include a husband and kids. Plans she hadn't bothered to fill him in on.

He'd been burned good. He didn't intend for it to happen again.

He pulled up in front of Adam's apartment.

'Hey,' Adam said, climbing in with a neon-green feather boa around his neck. 'Mind if we swing past the hospital on the way? Mel promised to lend this to a friend for a fancy-dress party and forgot to take it this morning. I told her we'd bring it by.'

Luke must have grimaced or something because when he glanced Adam's way, he was watching him. 'Problem?'

'No worries,' Luke said finally. He could smell Melanie's perfume on those feathers, as if she were in the car with them.

'What is it with you two?' Adam asked.

'We knew each other a few years back.' Luke checked his mirror, then eased into the traffic. 'It was kind of intense.'

'So that's why she was so moody this morning.' Adam leaned over to check out the stereo. 'This is one fine car.'

'Sure is.' Luke squinted into the afternoon sun-glare and concentrated on not thinking about how Melanie might have looked this morning. And not imagining how Melanie would look wearing nothing but that feather boa.

Five minutes later he pulled into the hospital's car park.

They slid out at the same time, Adam heading at a brisk pace for the hospital entrance, Luke content to cool his heels near the car. He didn't want to get involved in a conversation with Melanie. He didn't want to get involved, period.

His engineering contract had ended so he'd decided to catch up with his parents and friends, but on the eve of his departure from Dubai he'd been offered a partnership in a unique business opportunity. He was still considering. Returning overseas wouldn't go down well with his parents so as far as they were concerned he was settling in Sydney for good. Only Adam knew about the offer.

An impressive rounded bottom caught his eye in the next row of cars. Its owner was currently leaning into the engine of her car.

Tight black pants clung to long thighs and well-defined calf muscles. The quiet hum of lust in his veins was disturbed by a loud curse as the woman straightened, stamping a booted foot on the concrete.

Even as he said, 'Car trouble?' he recognised that voice, that thick rope of black hair over her shoulder. But anticipation forced the air out of his lungs, squeezing his chest and thickening his blood.

She whipped around, a flurry of colour and movement. 'Luke!' The multi-hued striped jumper suited her personality, suited the sparks that lit her eyes as their gazes connected. 'I was expecting Mikey.' She glanced at her watch. 'Any minute now.'

'What's the problem?' And who the hell was Mikey?

She shook her head as she rubbed her arms against the chill wind. 'Stupid thing won't start again. I think it's the battery.' Eyes wary, she waved him away when he would have stepped closer. 'It's okay, Mikey knows my car. He's my mechanic.'

So he knew her car. How well did Mikey-the-mechanic know Melanie? Judging by the sorry state of said vehicle, it would appear Mikey knew her quite well.

Luke turned his face into the wind and told himself he didn't need the distraction of Melanie in his life. He needed a home-and-hearth woman who'd give him those grandchildren his parents were always on about. Some day.

'You came with Adam, I assume? Did he bring my boa?'

Melanie's question forced him to turn back. He slid her a glance and his heart stalled at the sight. In that split second his hopes of finding a home-and-hearth type that packed half the punch Melanie did bottomed out. 'Yeah. He's just up ahead...' He pulled out his mobile, informed Adam, disconnected.

A moment later as he watched Adam approach, Luke fought a brief irrational stab of jealousy. Adam knew Melanie now, better than he did. He knew her idiosyncrasies, the scent she left in the bathroom after her shower. It was Adam who saw her mussed and sleepy-eyed first thing in the morning.

'Thanks,' she said as Adam draped the green feathers around her neck.

'Well.' Adam looked from Luke to Mel and back. 'You two want to—'

'I'm waiting for Mikey,' Mel said, a wealth of defiance in her tone as she flicked at the boa. 'Ah, there he is.' She waved the feathers to a yellow van cruising the parking lot. 'You two go ahead. I'll be fine.'

'You want to come for a drink too, Mel, when you get your car running?' Adam asked.

'Not tonight.'

Luke watched her eyes flicker with some emotion he couldn't identify, heard the hesitation and the tightness in her voice. 'Let me guess,' he drawled, holding those eyes. 'You have to wash your hair.'

'I have an appointment.' She didn't flinch or look away and was it his imagination or did her grey eyes turn sultry? 'I'm booked in for a massage and leg wax at six-thirty.'

Too much information. Too late, Luke recognised the danger and struggled to get past the image of her lying on a white couch, slippery, naked. With a strand of green feathers. Fingers of heat scored his skin. He shifted his stance to accommodate the building tension. He really, really didn't need to go any further down that track. 'Okay, then…'

He trailed off as he watched the sandy-haired Mikey climb out of his van and approach Melanie, a battery under one beefy arm and a swagger and a smile that didn't fool anyone.

Then he saw her smile back and his confidence in Mel's ability to see through men like that deflated like a lead balloon. 'If you need any help…' He directed his offer to no one in particular and set a beeline for his car. 'Call us. Where shall we go?' he asked Adam.

Adam turned to Luke, his shrewd blue eyes assessing. 'Somewhere quiet and comfortable where you can fill me in on your acquaintance with Melanie Sawyer.'

'Okay, girls, let's see what we've got.' Melanie tipped the contents of the shoebox onto the table and pushed up her sleeves.

She and two colleagues were down to sorting prizes and matching numbers in the hospital employees' cafeteria.

'This silent auction was a great idea, Mel.' Sophie spread out the cards with the donated prizes written on them.

'You bet,' Marie agreed with enthusiasm. 'We're going to raise some money for the Rainbow Road *and* have ourselves a good time.'

'Hopefully,' Sophie, ever the voice of caution, said.

'Where's your sense of adventure?' Mel looked at Sophie, the youngest and newest member of the fund-raising group. 'What's the worst that can happen? If things don't work out you end up home alone at ten p.m. on a Saturday night. Not too late to dial up pizza, open a bottle of wine and watch a DVD.' Like Luke, she thought, remembering the spark between them as she'd passed him his DVDs.

Instantly she was back in the past with Luke's mouth moving over her body, her hands in the silky strands of his hair as he took her higher, higher…

Her pulse took off God knew where and she must have taken after it, because when she finally focused on her surroundings her friends were watching her curiously.

She cleared her suddenly dry throat and said, 'The best part about being alone is you get to choose the movie.'

Marie shook her head. 'Sounds like a waste of a good Saturday night.'

'Not at all.' *Not when you've got nothing better to do.* Mel forced herself to straighten into business mode. 'We've sorted the prizes in order of value. We've got several full body massages and dinners, lots of dinners-and-movies. Now we're down to the serious prizes. A sunrise hot air balloon ride and champagne breakfast, tickets for a guided tour to the top of the Harbour Bridge followed by dinner at Doyles Seafood Palace— if you've still got an appetite, that is.'

'And your donation, Mel. A chauffeured limo to Ben and Carissa Jamieson's new hideaway in the Blue Mountains,' Marie read from the prize description. 'Romantic overnight for two, catered meals, all mod cons in a bush setting.' Marie's eyes flicked to Melanie. 'The sad thing is, come Saturday night you'll be the only one not enjoying yourself.'

'Who says I haven't got a hot date lined up already? Can we move along here?' she said, feeling a little of that heat creep up her neck at the lie. 'Some of us have to work in the morning.'

Bending her head to the task at hand, she concentrated on *not* feeling Marie's speculative eyes on her. 'The guys have been given a number and have written their bid alongside.' She spread the bids on the table. 'We order the numbers according to their bids, from highest to lowest, then match them to the prizes. No one knows their partner till Saturday night…oh, my God.' Melanie stared at the zeros on number twenty-seven.

'Ten thousand dollars,' Marie read out over her shoulder. 'Wow! Guess he takes your prize, huh, Mel?' She did the eyebrow thing again. 'Are you sure you don't want to include yourself in the deal? Snag yourself a rich stranger for the evening, like Carissa?'

'Quite sure.' Melanie did a mental head shake. Who could afford that kind of money on hospital wages? Except…some bids came from outside, from family and friends… *Luke's got money to burn.* Melanie's pulse did a quick one-two.

No, she assured herself. It was too late for Luke's bid. And Adam wouldn't meddle in the Rainbow Road's business. Would he?

CHAPTER THREE

BEN and Carissa's very new and private city escape might be only a couple of hours' drive from Sydney but it wasn't exactly Highway One. Mel frowned as she steered her car through the dense eucalypt forest and hoped its out-of-tune engine wouldn't give her any grief on the way home.

She glanced at the low scudding clouds then pumped up the heater and focused on beating the imminent cloudburst, wondering if the track Ben had generously called a road would still be there in three hours' time when her guest and his partner for the evening arrived.

Her very rich or very charitable guest. Who was he? She shook off the shiver that coasted down her spine. She'd do the meet-and-greet thing to ensure they had everything they needed for a perfect intimate evening before she left, and find out then.

Finally the track opened up into a cleared block. The recently constructed retreat stood on a rise, its full-length windows on three sides looked out onto bushland and the nearby mountains. But with the sky darkening every wintry minute, Melanie didn't pause to admire the view.

With her cartons of supplies precariously balanced and tucked beneath her chin, she made it to the door as the first needles of rain pricked at her face.

As she stepped inside her gaze took in the welcoming surroundings. Burgundy rugs covered the honeyed wooden floor, bold wall hangings lent warmth to the room. There was a stone fireplace with kindling and a beautiful baby grand piano by the window, waiting for Ben to compose.

Bedroom ready, she noted on her quick tour of inspection. There was a sumptuous bathroom and a separate spa and sauna.

Her first job was to light the fire and add some much-needed warmth. She lit the kindling, waited a moment, then added a couple of logs and watched as the flames sputtered and caught, filling the room with the scent of eucalypts.

Not knowing her guests' preferences, she'd prepared a choice of prawn cocktail or pumpkin soup, a gourmet beef casserole with green side salad and fresh home-baked bread, and individual sticky date puddings or strawberries with cream for dessert. Not bad for someone who hated cooking.

She slid the casserole into the oven to heat slowly, set the table with ruby-red candles and put a matching bottle of wine on the kitchen bench. Checked her watch for the umpteenth time. A couple of hours to kill before her guests were due to arrive.

There was no TV. Not a book in sight. Pacing in front of the windows and clicking her nails, she shook her head at the wind-tossed trees. She had to do *something*. Anything to soothe the tension that had grabbed her with iron fists the moment she'd recognised Luke—had it only been two days?—and hadn't let go.

A soak in that to-die-for bathroom? She could manage that and still have time on her hands.

Five minutes later she put on a favourite rock CD she'd found in Ben's collection and cranked the volume up. Then she immersed herself up to the neck in hot fragrant bubble bath.

Outside the rain drummed on the roof. The wind had picked up—she could hear the trees, the splash of water against the frosted window. If it got any heavier she might be the only one here for the evening. Not a bad prospect—a glass of red, a toasty fire…

When the water began to cool, the thought of that fire's

warmth held instant appeal, so, wrapping a towel around herself, she took her clothes to the living room to dress.

Early dusk shrouded the view outside, but the fire-glow was enough to see by. She opened the towel and sighed as her damp bath-softened skin welcomed the heat. Pure bliss.

She let the towel slide slowly from her fingers, down her body as she closed her eyes and absorbed the sensation. Turning, she let the flames' heat warm her back while she rolled her head in time to the beat of the music. Tugging her hair free, she tossed it over her shoulder as she belted out the lyrics.

Hardly aware at first, she began to move her hands. Over her collar-bones, down her sides to the curve of her waist, the firmness of her abdomen. She barely noticed the funky rhythm any more. It had been a long time since hands other than her own had touched her naked skin.

Luke's hands.

She slid her palms over her breasts, felt them grow heavy as her nipples tightened. Her flesh swelled and moistened, her blood thickened and the sweet pull of arousal tugged at her womanhood.

She could've got lucky tonight. She had no doubt whatsoever that the man who'd paid ten thousand dollars would've come to the party and eased the ache.

If she'd opted to be his partner.

Why couldn't she take her own advice and have a fling as she'd told Carissa to do? She had a drawerful of sexy underwear at home, something pretty to wear beneath that no-nonsense uniform she wore every day. The only guy who ever saw it was Adam when she did her laundry and he didn't count.

She turned and saw her reflection in the glass window. Her hands dropped to her sides. *What a sad sight you are, girl. And what are you doing?* Even if it was teeming with rain and there was no one living within a seven-kilometre radius and a car's lights would alert her to any arrivals…

A sudden shivery thrill rippled through her, as if someone had traced a fingernail down her body from neck to navel to…

Hands rising automatically to shield herself, she peered into the gloom. Nothing but rain. She'd been without a lover in too long, that was all, and seeing Luke again had reawakened those lustful thoughts.

She shook the feeling away and turned back to the fire, reached for her bra and panties that no one ever saw. She had a meal to check on, wine to uncork, a welcome smile to cultivate.

He was going to freeze his balls off out here. Probably a good thing, considering the naked woman on the other side of the glass was Melanie.

Shaking the moisture from his face, Luke hunched his shoulders inside his rain-soaked jumper as he stood several feet away in the sheltering dark of the dripping eucalypts. He could still feel the residual gut-punch that had knocked him off-centre when he'd seen her enter the living room, wrapped in nothing but a towel.

He'd taken that in his stride—it had, after all, been a big towel. Heat still prickled his skin and sweat tracked a path down his spine even as the rain soaked through his shirt and sweater. Then, by God, she'd had to go and drop the damn thing. Not drop exactly, more of a slide, like a gloved hand over porcelain.

But unlike any normal healthy male who hadn't had a woman in a while, he didn't watch. Nope. He didn't notice the way her breasts with their wine-dark nipples swayed in time with the music as she moved. He didn't see the tiny birthmark on her left buttock. He knew nothing about the way her hands moved over satin-smooth skin.

Hell.

He fisted his hands inside the pockets of his tailor-made woollen trousers and glared up at the sky, letting the rain pelt his face. Anything to cool the beat of his blood and block the image that continued to dance behind his eyes.

He could hardly knock now and alert Melanie to the fact

that he'd seen her naked and—he did a quick check—yep, she still was.

Never mind that he'd been standing here for five minutes hammering on the door *before* she'd appeared—a futile effort over that rock concert going on in there. And that he was probably going to catch pneumonia.

His hopes for a home-cooked meal and quiet evening of solitude going over his father's business accounts—well, it wasn't going to happen. Not after the temperature-elevating sight he'd witnessed. He scowled into the trees. Why had he let Adam talk him into this? Because a week ago he hadn't known Melanie was his flatmate, that was why.

He shouldn't have sent the limo away before he'd got inside. He should've brought an umbrella. And a spare pair of trousers. He should *not* have come an hour early.

Progress, he noted, glancing back over his shoulder. Finally. He breathed only marginally easier when he saw her reaching for her underwear. Her purple barely there underwear. The sight as she slid those panties up her thighs only added fuel to the fire in his blood.

When he looked again she was dressed and preparing something at the kitchen workbench, her hair a flow of ebony gleaming under the down-lights. For the first time he noticed the aromatic scent of something hot and spicy—red meat, onions, a hint of garlic.

He shook the water from his hair, sluiced it from his face with a hand and picked up his bag. Time to let her in on the surprise.

Melanie frowned at the door. Was that a knock? It was possible with the wind and music that she hadn't heard the limo pull up, but no lights had beamed through the windows, no doors had slammed shut. It looked dark and lonely and wild out there.

There it was again. A definite knock. More insistent. And no wonder—it was pouring.

She turned off the stereo on her way, slicked her hair over

her shoulder and, keeping the security chain on, she cracked open the door. The light shone on the figure of a big man glistening with water.

'Good evening.' Luke's voice.

Luke's face.

Luke's eyes fixed on hers, and looking...hot.

For a stunned second she couldn't move. Some part of her brain registered that he wasn't damp—he was soaked, and that there was no limo in sight. Desperation had her hoping for a reasonable explanation that didn't include him winning her prize.

But no. Shock waves of chills and heat chased through her body while he produced a card with a water-smudged number twenty-seven and held it out to her. 'Seems I won this retreat for the evening.'

Adam, I'm going to kill you. 'How did you get here?' A tight, breathless moan rose up her throat.

He jerked a thumb at the track. 'I let the ride go. Ah...I was... I'm a little early. Sorry.'

Which meant... Her whole body quivered with that implication as her eyes darted to his. 'How much too early?'

His eyes glistened with arousal...but it *could* have been a trick of the firelight or water dripping from his lashes, carving waterfalls in the creases bracketing his nose and mouth. Couldn't it?

Fat chance. She'd been caught out.

Oh, cripes, just let the man in. Her numb fingers slipped on the metal, rattling the chain as she slid it off and pulled the door wide.

She stood aside, wincing as his shoes made squelchy noises on the floor. Their gazes remained locked as he toed them off. His expression was too carefully schooled to be anything but contrived. He'd obviously been stumbling around in the dark for the past...*how long?* On further consideration she decided she didn't want to know.

Her eyes left his to take a slow and thorough inventory of

the damage. 'You need to get out of those wet things. You do have a change of clothes...don't you?' In that slim business case? He'd brought a *business* case to a romantic rendezvous? Except that he'd come alone, a fact that was only now seeping through the brain fog.

'I'm afraid not.' Grim-faced, he raked a hand through his hair, scattering droplets.

'There's a clothes dryer, they'll be dry in no—'

'Forget it, it's wool and an old favourite.'

When she looked up he'd already hauled the steel blue jumper and shirt over his head, leaving his chest gleaming in the foyer's down-lights. Rugged, bronzed, slick with water.

She glanced behind her. 'There's a towel around here somewhere...' Anything to cover that glorious nakedness.

'Got it.'

On the floor behind the couch, out of sight and right where she'd left it. Of course, he already knew that. Her face burned anew. Not that she had any hang-ups about nudity, but remembering the little fantasy she'd been playing in her mind and knowing the object of that fantasy had been watching...

'And the trousers?' She let her gaze move over the dark fabric, and imagined how it would feel, how *he* would feel beneath her hand now, five years on. Tried not to think about other times when she'd done just that.

'Wool too. Dry-clean only.'

His voice, thick and strained, brought her eyes back to his. It could have been because he was wet and cold and wishing he were somewhere else, but—dear heaven—she'd seen more than enough down there.

'The bathroom.' She pointed the way. 'There are a couple of robes behind the door, then bring your wet clothes back here and put them in front of the fire.'

Her pulse roared like thunder in her ears. No, not her pulse, she realised, when she saw him glance outside on his way to the bathroom. An approaching storm front.

'Great,' she muttered as unease added to the volatile mix of emotions churning through her. Driving home in this weather on an unfamiliar road—track, she amended—was going to be an adventure she wasn't looking forward to.

But she had a job to finish before she could escape. Stir the casserole, butter the rolls, *get a grip*.

The sound of the water running in the shower had her hands pausing on the expensive bottle of wine she'd uncorked. She would *not* think of all that golden skin and wet, gleaming muscle. Those large hands, soap, steam and warm, slippery moisture.

She concentrated instead on filling the crystal wineglass without spilling it. If she hadn't faced the prospect of the long ride ahead she'd have poured herself one. Instead she breathed in the full-bodied aroma and took a generous sip from Luke's glass, set it down and finished dinner preparations as the storm rumbled closer.

She didn't put on the romantic piano CD or light the candles as she'd intended. Obviously they were going to be wasted on Luke and they certainly didn't need any reminders of the past.

Which had her wondering why he hadn't married one of those beautiful women she'd seen him with and had those children he'd always wanted.

His father had made it quite clear that was what he expected when he'd answered the one and only phone call she'd ever made to Luke, a month after they'd parted ways.

Luke's mobile number had no longer worked, and, desperate to contact him, she'd phoned his parents' home. She'd been so relieved when his father had answered her long-distance call from Coffs Harbour.

'Melanie?' he said in a voice so like Luke's, her heart turned over in her chest. Then a silence so long she thought they'd been disconnected. 'Ah, the waitress.'

The scorn in his voice lanced through her like a skewer through a cocktail kebab. 'Please, I need to contact him; it's very important.'

'With girls like you it always is.' She heard the unmistakable annoyance, the scepticism in his voice.

Melanie hugged her arms and stared at the black windows, remembering in horrible detail her fear, the overwhelming sense of aloneness, the frustration of being stopped at the gate, so to speak. So close yet so far.

'I need to speak to Luke,' she repeated.

'He's not interested in any further contact with you. Why don't you save yourself the trouble and just let it go?'

So with no alternative, she had. A few months later she'd resigned herself to never seeing Luke again, a year later her application into the Bachelor of Nursing course had been accepted and she'd started over with a new career and a new outlook on life.

But like the storm, those dark memories had encroached on the room, sucking away the warmth of the fire. A flash of lightning lit up the scene as Luke entered the living room in the thick bathrobe with his wet clothes in his hands.

His overpowering, masculine energy, like a magnetic field, radiated across the room, dragging the breath clean out of her lungs. What she could see of his skin beneath the smattering of springy chest hair gleamed bronze and inviting against the snowy white towelling, a temptation that had her hands curling in reflex.

No. She forced her hands to straighten, smoothed her damp palms over her jeans. She wasn't going down that track again.

Their eyes met while her heart drummed like the rain on the roof. Dark eyes, dark gaze. But for a beat of time, a warmer hot chocolate gaze that melted her from the inside out, thawing the chill of the past few moments. The way he'd looked at her so many times before.

But his father's words rang in her ears, as loud and clear as the day he'd said them. *The waitress.* She might have pulled herself up a ways, but she was, and always would be, the hired help's daughter.

Apart from the sex, she wasn't in his league. It made it easier to turn away, to gather up her belongings in the living room. To ignore the sensation of Luke's eyes burning through her as she shrugged into her coat while he leaned against the back of the couch.

She pulled her keys out of her pocket. 'The dinner's ready when you are. I've left a menu on the bench, the makings for breakfast are in the fridge, so I'll be...' She trailed off under his harsh gaze.

'You're not thinking of driving in this, are you?'

As if to punctuate his words, lightning stabbed through the window, followed immediately by a crack that shook the house on its foundations.

She matched his glare with one of her own. 'I can't stay here.' *With you naked under that robe. With five years of lone-liness and frustration chipping away at my will-power.* She turned away and began walking towards the door. 'I have to get home.'

'I saw the state of the track and that was a good hour ago,' he said, and she felt the air move as he dumped his clothes on the couch. 'No streetlights till you hit sealed road, maybe not even then. No one to lend a hand if you get bogged.'

She swung back to face him. 'I've got my mobile phone.'

'Don't be ridiculous, Mel. Surely we can manage to share a meal and a fire without...'

Tearing each other's clothes off? Ah, yes, exactly what he'd been going to say, Mel thought, watching the tell-tale line of colour etch his cheekbones, feeling the flare of response smouldering in her own traitorous body.

She let out a slow breath. 'Okay.'

It wasn't one of Carissa's 'signs'—*it wasn't*—but she could do this; they could do this. Two intelligent, civilised adults could share an evening, no problem. If she didn't dim the lights and use the candles, if she stuck to the rock CD or no music at all—if she didn't look at him—they'd do fine.

She could retire to the second bedroom after tea, catch up

on some much needed rest, and in the morning this whole get-away retreat thing would be over and the Rainbow Road would be ten thousand dollars richer.

CHAPTER FOUR

'WILL anyone worry if you don't come home tonight?'

His voice took on a low, husky sound and all manner of scenarios involving her and Luke and why she wouldn't be home tonight danced into Melanie's mind. She slammed a mental lid on that Pandora's box and shook her head.

'No. I stay over at Carissa's sometimes. Adam and I don't keep tabs on each other.' She gestured at the bench. 'Your dinner. I'll let you get on with it.'

'Alone?'

The breath caught in her throat as the unspoken message in his smoky voice shivered through her, as the lambent heat in his eyes sent her pulse sky-rocketing. 'You obviously intended solitude,' she pointed out.

'When circumstances change—' he shrugged '—hardly seems fair that the cook goes hungry after all the trouble she went to.'

Circumstances had changed all right. Which was why she was stuck here for now, alone with Luke Delaney.

Resigned, and, yes, hungry, she slipped her keys back in her pocket, shrugged off her coat and moved to the small kitchen area off the living room. 'Why don't you try the wine while I get the seafood? We can eat by the fire, it's warmer there.'

And she didn't need to face Luke in a robe across the intimate table setting with its scented candles and vase of violets. She took the cocktails out of the fridge and set them on the bench.

'Here you go.' The husky sound of his voice made her jump.

She hadn't heard Luke come up behind her and jerked around, almost knocking the two wineglasses from his hands.

It was easier—but safer—to look straight ahead at the large, blunt fingers curled around the delicate crystal stem…and on that soft V of the robe…than to tip her head back and meet his eyes.

He smelled of soap and new fabric and if she leaned closer her lips would meet warm, masculine skin just above that V. She remembered in full detail the exact spot where her lips touched his body when they stood toe to toe. Thigh to thigh. Breast to chest.

Oh, boy. Not so safe after all.

She tried to ignore her body's toe-curling, lip-tingling response and took the glass with a murmured, 'Thank you,' and stepped back.

Except that now she could see the masculine texture of his jaw, the fullness of his lips and the dark stillness in his eyes, like a deep river with hidden depths and mysteries.

She took a sip to moisten her suddenly parched throat and watched him do the same. Watched his Adam's apple bob as he swallowed. *Oh, stop.* Watching, staring, admiring. Remembering.

'Why don't you—' *get out of my space, you're crowding me* '—go make yourself comfortable and I'll bring the food.'

Her fingers tightened around the glass. The storm's ferocity matched the beat of her heart, the stunning impact of his gaze while he took another gulp.

'Give me your glass, then.' He took it from her numb fingers, then turned and carried both glasses to the living area while she remained on the other side of the bench.

'Prawn cocktails coming right up.' She huffed out a breath, angry that her voice sounded breathless and weak. 'Steady,' she ordered herself quietly. 'No more confined spaces.'

When she moved to the living area he was crouched in front of the fire, feeding it another log. She took the opportunity to put their prawns on the coffee-table and sink onto the safety of an armchair.

There'd been nights like these when they'd shared their passion in front of an open fire in Luke's parents' house on cool summer evenings. Grossly unnecessary in mid-January, but oh-so-romantic. He was remembering too—she knew by the silence, so tense she swore she could hear it snapping over the drumming of the rain.

Big mistake. The fireplace wasn't any safer than the table setting.

Then the lights flicked once and went out. Blackness and tension suddenly filled the room, relieved only by the flames. She held her breath as Luke stood and turned to her, eyes glittering in the reflected glow.

'Well, I guess that takes care of any paperwork I planned to do.'

'I wonder how long it will be?' Mel shivered. It felt even more isolated, more confining, more dangerous now. The world had shrunk to the ruddy sphere of firelight and she leaned instinctively towards it. Towards Luke.

'Could be hours.' He reached for one of the silver compotes and sat down on the leather couch across from her.

When she just stared at him, amazed at his casual attitude, he shrugged. 'Might as well eat.'

Melanie tried, but her stomach was too tight with nerves to swallow more than the first couple of mouthfuls. Luke on the other hand suffered no such problem.

Twenty minutes later he'd finished a healthy serving of her casserole and started on the sticky date pudding. Apart from brief comments about the food, when the rain might ease, whether they had enough wood inside to last, hardly a word passed between them.

Yet Melanie could feel the tension. It hummed in the air, louder than the rain's rhythm on the roof, the hiss of the fire, more powerful than the wind whipping around the windows.

'So what papers were you going to work on?' she asked. Anything to drown that lack of normal human conversation.

'Just some of Dad's finances. I promised I'd take a look. Thought I might as well start tonight.'

'You're staying a while, then? In Sydney?'

'Yes.' He stopped scraping the bottom of his dessert bowl to look at her. 'It's a big city, Mel.'

'Not so big. You're Adam's friend.'

'Our paths don't have to cross. Unless you want them to.' He set the bowl on the coffee-table and watched her as long, tension-filled seconds ticked by.

Waiting for a response? Her heart stalled, then kaboomed once.

'We're adults,' he said, when she didn't answer. 'We can bury the past and try to get along.'

'Do we really ever bury the past?'

He scrubbed at his jaw. 'Not all, I guess. For example...'

He rose in one quick agile movement that had Melanie scooting upright, pulse stepping up a notch, hands gripping the chair.

But he didn't come near her. He retrieved his briefcase from the near the door, padded back to the fire and unsnapped it, pulled out a packet of marshmallows resting on his notes.

'I was going to toast these tonight. Seeing you again the other day reminded me I hadn't enjoyed them in too long.' He studied her a moment and she knew he knew she was remembering. 'I wanted to see if they still taste the same.'

For a moment she could almost taste them on her tongue, could almost taste *him*—warm and deliciously tempting.

'How about it? We'll need a couple of thin branches, won't take a moment...'

'No!' Her instant jolt of reaction was premature. A quick trip outside would give her a few moments alone. Time to cool the slow-combustion energy building between them. 'I'll do it,' she said, and pushed up. 'You get that robe wet and...' Well, they both knew what that meant...

She took her coat from the hat-stand by the door and let herself outside. The rain had paused briefly but the gums dripped, the air was redolent with eucalyptus and wet earth, cooling her heated skin, but not cold enough to cool the hot pulse of blood in her veins.

Was she seriously entertaining the prospect of sharing something as cosy as a fire and toasted marshmallows with Luke Delaney? For one insane moment Melanie fingered the car keys in her pocket and considered getting into her car and driving as fast and as far away as she could. Away from temptation, away from the memories.

Not so insane, she thought, more like self-protection.

She should lock herself in the other bedroom and pull the covers over her head and stay there till morning. Except that was the coward's way out and she liked to think she was no coward. And an insistent part of her brain nagged her to find out more about what he'd been doing since they parted.

Luke snatched the decision from her when the door opened and he peered out into the darkness, his body silhouetted against the glow inside.

'Yeah, yeah, I'm coming.' She grabbed a branch, shook off the moisture and hurried to the door. 'Strip this and I'll make hot chocolate.'

'I'll make the drinks. You've done a first-rate job of the meal, now it's my turn.'

He didn't look at the branch she held. He was looking at her scooped neckline. An entirely different kind of strip teased its way through her senses. But it must have been her imagination. When his eyes finally lifted to hers they were dark and calm, not the eyes of a man entertaining thoughts of heat and hands and naked bodies.

She nodded as a remnant of that hot flash seeped into her blood. 'Okay, kitchen's all yours.'

His size and proximity to the door didn't make it easy to get back inside. She had to slip past him, her shoulder brushing the firm muscles beneath his robe. Even with two layers of clothing between them deadly temptation snaked through her body as she carried the branch and sat cross-legged in front of the fire, feeding it damp leaves that released a curl of spitting eucalyptus-fragrant smoke.

When he returned a few minutes later, mugs in hand, the whole room smelled of the Aussie outdoors. He set the mugs on the table and dropped a marshmallow in each while she threaded two marshmallows onto the stick the way they used to. She handed him the branch, refusing to look at the melted chocolate heat in his eyes. Preferring the much safer chocolate in the mug as she took it from the table.

'What have you been doing for the past few years?' she asked, desperately searching for something to say. 'I hear you've been quite successful.'

His expression turned enigmatic. 'Depends on what you mean by success. If you're referring to my work, then, yes, I've done okay.'

'Adam told me you were in Dubai. That's a long way from home.'

He shrugged. 'What's home when you have no ties?'

'What about your parents? They're not ties?'

'Of course they are, but if Dad had his way I'd be a partner in his business, married and giving him grandkids by now.'

He turned and shrugged a smile. For a heartbeat she saw the ghosts of lost dreams, like silent shadows reflected by the fire.

'The world's my workplace now,' he continued. 'I'm good at what I do—engineering geologists are always in demand, especially in the developing world.'

'I thought you took that job in Queensland…?' *The one you left me behind for.*

He nodded. 'The best decision I ever made. It opened doors. If I hadn't taken that job when I did, I wouldn't be where I am today career-wise.'

'I'm glad, Luke.'

If his father had put her in touch with him, if she'd told him the truth, maybe he'd never have gone overseas. In a way it had been worth the angst, the pain, to know he'd made it.

But regret lodged tight in her chest for what she'd given up. Perhaps the wine had made her maudlin, bringing those old memories to the surface again.

'Yeah. Well.' He rotated the branch with its two pink marsh-mallows in a loose grip as he gazed into the fire. 'Guess we both got what we wanted.'

Everything inside Melanie rebelled at his throw-away line. She opened her mouth, then pressed her lips together tight against the urge to deny it, but some sound must have escaped because he slid her a glance, one eyebrow raised.

'You *did* get what you wanted, didn't you, Mel?'

She bit the inside of her mouth. Told herself it didn't matter what he thought. She knew the truth, she'd tried to do the right thing, and that was enough.

'How was the trip up north?' His eyes returned to the fire as he rotated the branch with maddening care. 'Hot days, balmy tropical nights...'

Desperate days, *lonely* nights. She screwed her eyelids shut to stop the sting of tears. His assumption was way off base. An image flashed before her—Luke and her making love, their limbs twined together, mouths feasting, hearts in sync. *Damned* if she was going to let him think she jumped into bed with the next available guy to come along.

'Stop right there!' She slammed a fist into the couch.

She saw his hand still, tighten, his posture stiffen. Smelled the scent of burning sugar as the marshmallow turned black. Like what was left of their relationship.

'Things didn't pan out the way you wanted?' His sarcastic tone blew through her like the storm-lashed evening as he tossed the smouldering branch into the fire.

In the silence that followed, she heard a shower of sparks in the fireplace, the spit of rain against the window as the storm picked up again. Finally he turned, the fire reflecting in his sharp brown eyes as he watched her. Accusing? Assessing? Condemning?

Yet he was the one with the sexual magnetism and the wealth and power to make sure it happened with any woman he fancied. 'Don't tell me you haven't been with a woman in five years.' She watched the flicker of admission in those eyes and wanted to cry. Hugging her arms against the stab of jealousy, she met his gaze. 'I wrote to you.'

The instant the words were out, her heart tumbled inside her ribcage and she cursed her too-hasty tongue. Now she watched for a reaction. Any reaction that would tell her whether he received it—a business-sized envelope, name typed, no return info on the back.

She felt the immediate change in the atmosphere, the abrupt shift in tension as Luke straightened, the creases between his brows deepening. Watching her differently now through narrowed eyes. 'When?'

'A few weeks later. I sent it to your parents' address.'

His eyes flickered once before he blanked all expression. 'I never got it.'

Because they never forwarded it. 'I always wondered.'

'Why?'

'Because I never got a—'

'Why did you write?'

She looked into the eyes of the man who'd changed her life for ever. 'Because your mobile phone number didn't work, my emails bounced back. It was my last hope.'

His expression sharpened further, his lips pulling tight as he worked through her words. 'Last hope?' His voice was harsh, derisive. 'If it had been that important you could've tried the next logical step of contacting my parents by phone.'

Oh, how she burned to tell him, but what good would it do now? He was obviously back here to reconnect with them and no way did she want to sabotage that. She'd have given anything to have her own parents back; their deaths had rocked her world. No, she simply couldn't do it.

Anyway, who would he believe—a five-minute lover or his father? No contest. So she gave him a deliberately vague shrug. 'I…wanted to make sure it was over between us.'

'I thought you made yourself perfectly clear on that last night.'

Her body suddenly felt drained and limp and she had to stop herself from reaching out to touch him, to absorb some of his strength, to tell him. 'I took your non-reply as your answer.'

His jaw clenched, he closed his eyes briefly. 'I'm sorry.' He reached for the barely touched bottle of wine still on the table from dinner and poured himself a full glass. 'I stepped straight into a promotion and was overseas a month after I'd started in Queensland. I changed my phone number and my email address.'

And didn't give me another thought. 'Yeah, well, it's all rain down the drain now.'

She watched him raise the crystal, sparking in the firelight, its ruby liquid caress his upper lip a moment before he drank.

She heard him swallow, felt her own throat tighten in response. If she leaned closer…would that potent blend of heat and wine and Luke still taste the same? Still lead her down that same dizzy, out-of-control course? Or, in this case, to that warm and tempting king size bed a few quick steps from here?

She picked up her mug, wrapped her stiff fingers around it and tried to sip the chocolate, but there was a lump in her throat and it wasn't the marshmallow. It was resentment, hard and bitter and impossible to swallow.

Ignoring his own mug, Luke drank the rest of his wine, poured himself another. Mel started to warn him he'd pay for it in the morning but instantly bit down on her words. If he wanted to get quietly drunk that was his business. Cripes, she was almost tempted to join him, but someone needed to be alert if the storm did any more damage.

So she leaned back and let her lips caress the china. What would Carissa make of all this? Oh, she knew already what her stepsister would say and she was sick of hearing about signs and fate and soul mates. Which was why she hadn't told Carissa about Luke's return yet.

Well, the official part of the evening was over. Hostess duties were way over. 'I'm going to bed,' she said, pushing up off the couch.

He turned slowly and met her eyes and the moment sizzled with possibilities. It didn't help that his robe had parted. Firelight stroked the contours of his chest with flickering shadow and bronze.

Her skin tightened, her blood heated, and in that tension-filled silence, broken only by the snap and crackle of the fire, she noticed that the wind had dropped. That the rain was only a soft sibilance of sound on the roof.

That his eyes held the same intense awareness she knew hers held.

They'd be sleeping those few quick steps from each other. If they wanted, they could take all this tempting heat, the restless throbbing, the aching anticipation and light another kind of fire.

While she held her breath he continued watching her as if weighing that decision in his mind, then said, 'Thanks for the meal, Melanie. Goodnight.' He turned away to look back into the fire.

That breath whooshed out. 'Goodnight.' With one of the fat candles in her hand, she walked to the bedroom, closed the door softly behind her. Then shook her head. No toothbrush, no pyjamas. She took off her trousers and jumper and crawled between the sheets in her underwear, then blew out the candle.

The chill of the linen against her hot skin made her shiver. Awareness chased over her body as surely as if he stood watching her. She knew he was thinking about her alone in this white-on-white bedroom. That he was wondering if she'd stripped bare. Her nipples puckered beneath the satin bra, she couldn't seem to stop her legs from moving. Closing her eyes, she willed herself to try to sleep. An impossibility.

CHAPTER FIVE

IT WAS still dark when Melanie opened her eyes again. Her mouth was dust dry and she needed the bathroom. She found her jumper in the grey light beyond the window, pulled it on and crept to the door. A chink of light glowed as she inched it open and made her way quietly to the living area.

The fire had burned low but there was enough light to see Luke asleep on the big leather couch, the empty wine bottle and an open bottle of gin on the coffee-table. He'd found Ben's liquor cabinet. Which meant he'd be out cold. She checked her watch by firelight, blinked in amazement. Three a.m. She'd managed to sleep a good five hours.

She used the bathroom then returned to the kitchen. The tap hissed, preternaturally loud in the silence as she filled a glass. She drank it down, refilled it, then took it with her through the living area on her way back to bed. And paused. Just to check, she told herself. Night duty and checking on sleeping patients was ingrained into her life.

Luke was stretched out on his back, all long, masculine limbs and hard, honed body. The edges of his robe had fallen apart long ago. He'd left his briefs on, thank God. The hard curve of his jaw seemed softer, relaxed, and she longed to smooth her palm against it and feel the texture. His lips were slightly apart, as if waiting for hers.

She bit her own lips to stop the tingling. If things had been different, that was probably just what she'd be doing about now. Locking lips with Luke.

Shaking herself into action, she cast a quick eye around the room for a throwover. He might look hot, but conscience wouldn't allow her to walk away from a sleeping body without offering the comfort of a blanket.

Luke knew she was there, but right now he couldn't summon up anything even remotely physical. He was trapped in an uncooperative body that refused to allow him even the pleasure of watching her watch him.

His head pounded, his throat burned. He was never going to drink to excess again. He thought he might just be able to ask for a glass of water. He lifted one eyelid. Couldn't manage two.

And there she was. Nurse Nightingale with a glass of water in one hand and a blanket in the other. In her sweater and purple panties with those mile-long pale legs she looked as cool as the crystal-clear liquid he craved. And if she'd come closer he knew she'd be as warm and soft as that very welcome blanket.

On a low groan that seemed to come with no assistance from him, he started to raise his head, but someone was hammering it to the couch. 'Hey, Mel.' He sounded pathetic and he knew from previous experience she was going to tell him so.

But she took a hasty step back, her eyes wide and stunned. 'You're awake.'

Unfortunately, yes. He forced his rubber tongue to work. 'You wouldn't have a couple painkillers round here to go with that water, would you?'

She looked down as if surprised to find the glass in her hand. 'Oh, this is for— I thought you were asleep. I'll go check the first-aid box.'

'Thanks.' He closed the eye, almost sighed with relief as he felt the mohair blanket settle over his body.

An indeterminate time later cool hands lifted his head, two pills were placed on his tongue, then a glass raised to his lips. A gentle voice near his ear murmured, 'Swallow.'

With a supreme effort he raised himself up on an elbow

and carefully took the glass from her hand, wrapped his own clumsy fingers around it. For God's sake, he could do it himself. He hoped.

She smelled like the fresh green of spring but underlying that was the familiar scent of her skin. A scent he'd never been able to rid his senses of. Her eyes—when he focused—weren't the serves-you-right ones he expected, but soft with sympathy and something like understanding.

Not Melanie the girl who'd loved a good booze-up but any overindulgence on his part had meant he was history until he recovered.

This was Melanie the Nurse.

'More,' she urged when he would have stopped to stare into her wondrous grey eyes, to forget his discomfort a moment and immerse himself in those depths.

Light fingers traced his brow. 'You're dehydrated.' She made a clucking sound against her teeth. 'I'd've thought you'd have gotten past this by now.'

The reason for his binge mine-blasted through him, the pounding in his skull increased. 'Your news about the letter and trying to contact me.' Not that it changed anything now. 'I never kn—'

'Shh.' Her breath was warm and sweet against his face as she took the empty glass and let him lie back, murmuring something about tension and rest, a soothing wash of sound that seemed to seep into his bones. He closed his eyes.

'Remember that time you threw up at Janice's party?' she said, sliding an arm beneath his head and propping him up.

'How could I forget? You took off and left me there.'

'I shouldn't have. I'm sorry.'

Before his sluggish brain could react, she was on the couch beside him. Behind him. Her warmth surrounded him like the blanket as she slid her body beneath his so that his head was cradled against her belly, her legs on either side of him.

His whole body tensed, sensation streaked over his skin and

the old longing burned bright in his heart. Then he surrendered with a sigh of surprise and sheer pleasure.

'That's it. Relax.' Her voice was a calming whisper against his ear. He remembered other times when her whispers had been hoarse and demanding. This was a layer to Melanie that she'd never revealed. Perhaps she'd not known she had it back then. Or for her own reasons, she'd not shown it to him.

Her fingers massaged lazy circles on his temples, drawing away the pain, then worked through his hair to knead the base of his skull, easing away the tension.

'That perfume…'

'I'm not wearing any. Unless it's the bubble bath I had earlier.'

The one she'd had before he arrived, he thought hazily as she dug her thumbs deep into his neck. *Oh, yeah.* He groaned. *Right there.* He damn near lifted off the couch in bliss.

'Easy,' she said, a hint of amusement in the softly spoken word. 'This is strictly professional.'

'You can be professional with me any time you like.'

What might have been a ripple of laughter was nothing but a whisper against his brow, but it was powerful enough to fan the slow burning in his gut, to suck the air from his lungs. To distract him from the throbbing in his brain to another more insistent throbbing in his groin.

Which only made him more aware that nothing but a strip of satin separated his head from the smooth female flesh of her belly.

The best, and worst kind of torture. Hot with need, restless with longing—unwilling and unable to act on it. Knowing it might never happen. 'Melanie…'

Her fingers touched his lips. 'Sleep.'

'No. I need to tell you…' He tried to push up, but was held down by a firm hand. 'I should have left a forwarding address. With Carissa…'

He felt the hand curl and tighten into a fist against him. 'But you didn't,' she said, softly.

Surprised at the depth of emotion in her voice, he forced his eyes open, tilted his head back, and was disturbed to read that same intensity in her eyes.

Then it was gone, blanked out. She huffed a breath, disturbing the hair at his temples. 'We were good together while it lasted.'

'I—'

The decisive slash of her hand stirred the air. 'Just a fling. Leave it, Luke. Go back to sleep.'

Because he didn't want to deal with their past fuzzy-headed and sluggish with alcohol, he closed his eyes. *Just a fling*. It should have relieved him. But as he slipped into unconsciousness he didn't feel relief. He felt regret.

When Luke woke in the watery morning light he became aware of two things simultaneously. His headache had gone. Melanie hadn't. Somehow she'd extricated herself from behind without disturbing him and now lay alongside—he could feel the tangle of long limbs and hair.

Entwined was probably a more apt—and disturbing—description, since one of her arms was flung over his chest, her legs snug up against his. He let out a slow breath and kept very, very still. Two king-size beds to choose from and they were stretched out on a sofa barely wide enough for one.

How many times had he fantasised about waking up like this? With Melanie's body pressed against him, her face inches from his, her breath warm in his ear?

He opened his eyes slowly, checked to see if she was still asleep. Yep. Inky lashes resting on perfect ivory-coloured skin. Breathing slow and even.

But not for long. She shifted, a frown creasing her brow as she snuggled closer, away from the cold edge of the couch. He shifted too, against the torturous slide of her knee as it moved closer to dangerous territory. Her fingers, curled into the lapel of his robe, flexed and tightened. She'd always been a messy sleeper, he remembered. Even in sleep she couldn't stay still.

Outside, the birds' dawn chorus rang through the bush. A red glow tinted the fireplace, the room was still warm. Melanie must have added more fuel before she'd fallen asleep. Another disturbing thought—how long had she watched him through the night?

Turnabout was fair play, he decided, and looked at her again, torturing himself with what he couldn't have, couldn't touch. At least not the way he wanted to touch. He had most of the blanket, a plus since it gave him the opportunity to look his fill at the smooth curve of a naked thigh and hip with its sexy strip of purple lace.

On the downside, her jumper covered the rest of her, leaving him to remember what he'd seen beneath it last night. But her face—still the same. What would she do if he traced that delicate bone structure with his lips? With his tongue? If he kissed her now on that wide sleep-softened mouth?

Her lashes flickered. Grey eyes met his, first in confusion, then awareness.

He couldn't stop himself—he reached out and smoothed a strand of hair behind her ear. 'Good morning.'

'Hi.'

Her husky voice sent a torrent of heat through his body. It didn't help that she stretched languorously, sliding those sinuous legs against his. She stopped abruptly, the knowledge of what she was doing—to him, to herself—dark and smouldering in her eyes.

'I…guess I fell asleep too.'

He could feel her pulling away, physically and emotionally. Without thinking he reached out, curled a hand around her nape. Saw wariness sharpen her sleepy gaze. 'I guess you did. Thanks for being my guardian angel last night.'

Before she could answer, he closed those inches between them and laid his lips on hers. Sparks, heat, the quick flare of lust, the slower burn of something remembered, something deeper.

A few stunned seconds passed, then her mouth went pliant

beneath his. He felt the faint shiver run through her body and his own jerked in response. Oh, yeah, they still had it. That same recognition, that same magnetic attraction that had drawn him across the crowded function centre the instant he'd laid eyes on her again at his father's cocktail party.

He sifted the silky waterfall of hair through his fingers. Natural and easy to shift atop her, holding her prisoner against his burgeoning need. Damp heat to heat, hard against yielding, male to female.

Then he felt her hand against his chest, heard the muffled sound in her throat. His primitive instincts howled in protest as he pulled back to search her eyes. Enough time to see the light of passion fade to that wariness again.

He felt a sudden stab of loss and stroked her cheek. 'It's okay, Mel, it's just a kiss.'

'It's never "just a kiss" with you, Luke. You wipe my mind, make me forget.'

She wasn't the only one forgetting, he tried to remind himself as he moved closer again, but she rolled out of his arms off the couch, scrambling up and leaving him grasping thin air.

'You make me forget…everything,' she whispered, touching her mouth.

'Why is that a bad thing?' he said, not understanding why words that should flatter his male ego sounded more like a rejection. A rejection he'd be a darn sight better off accepting than fighting.

'I'm different now, we both are.'

'You never know, that might work for us. It was working fine a moment ago.'

For another moment she met his gaze, an honest and open longing that echoed deep in his gut, then as if she'd flicked a switch her expression changed. Unseen shadows prowled the space that had been humming with promise. She hugged her arms and turned away. 'I don't think so.'

'Why not?' he couldn't resist asking.

'I work full-time and then some. The kids need me. I don't have any time for…anything else.'

A lie. He watched the slim, stiff length of her. Even though he knew she'd felt that same passion he had moments ago, for some reason she didn't want to renew their relationship. *Neither do you. You've been flying solo over three continents and doing fine.* Why dig up the past now?

Except… He was a geologist—he liked digging. And he'd seen the truth in her eyes; it wasn't work that was stopping her. He needed to know why she'd refused him. And he'd always loved a challenge.

To avoid Luke's penetrating gaze she could feel boring holes in her back, Melanie pinned her gaze on the view outside. She barely noticed the first rays of thin sunlight spark off the wet leaves, barely heard the kookaburra's happy laugh.

She couldn't renew her relationship with Luke—because he wouldn't want one when she told him the whole story. Nor did they stand a chance at anything deeper than what they'd had. Luke was for fun times. Nothing more.

The man whose gaze had shifted from her back and was currently massaging the exposed length of her naked legs. If they hadn't been recently waxed the hairs would have been standing on end. She remained still, heard the slide of skin on fabric and the faint chink as he picked up the glass, the audible swallow, the plunk as he set it down.

She turned. 'I'll make breakfast as soon as I'm dressed.' She fought the female reaction as his eye massage continued. Only now it was her nipples rising under the intensity. 'The limo will be here to pick you up at ten.'

He lifted his eyes to hers. 'That's three hours away—cancel it. I'll drive back with you.'

She shook her head. She didn't need the extra distraction. 'I've got to clean up. I was going to come back later and do it, this way it's saved me a trip. You don't need to hang around and wait.' And watch.

'It's not going to take three hours to clean up. We can explore the property before we go.'

'In those shoes?'

He glanced at his damp but expensive leather shoes by the fireplace. 'I've got two more pairs at home. Come on, a quick jog. Guaranteed to warm you up.'

As if she needed warming up! 'I'm on duty at three-fifteen. And when I'm finished I'm going to crash for twelve hours or so, before I get up and do it all over again.'

'Don't you get time off for good behaviour?'

'Tuesday.' Bad move, telling him, she realised. 'I'm meeting some colleagues to decide how best to use the money we raised.' She just hadn't advised those colleagues yet. 'Excuse me, I'm going to dress.' As she escaped into the bedroom, leaving him to do the same, she heard him mutter something about a cold shower.

In the end, Melanie cancelled the limo because Luke threatened to follow her all the way back to Sydney to make sure her car didn't get bogged and it saved some money that she could put towards the Rainbow Road.

Conversation was kept to a minimum thanks to the dangerous road conditions and the ominous sound of the car's engine and the fact that Luke looked as if he was still suffering the side-effects of alcohol and lack of sleep.

Sitting in still-damp clothes probably didn't help. Nor did the knowledge that the fire hadn't been the only heat source that had warmed things up last night.

It simmered in the air between them, reminding her of how good he looked in firelight with the flames reflecting in his dark eyes, the burnished glow of his skin.

Hot.

She shoved up her sleeves, drew in a breath of overheated air and switched on the ancient demister. Her steamy thoughts were fogging up the windscreen.

They cooled, however, when she turned into his parents' street. She remembered. The fireside love-ins, the shared showers slippery with soap and sex. Luke's big mahogany bed and Egyptian sheets…

By the time she pulled up outside the elegant two-storey home with its circular drive and landscaped gardens, the steam had turned to a ball of ice in her stomach.

It didn't budge when his gaze searched her face—was he actually thinking of asking her in? No. She breathed a sigh of relief when he reached down for his briefcase.

He turned to her as he opened the door. 'Thanks for everything.'

Hard to miss the subtle message there. Hard to meet his eyes and *not* react to the intensity.

'Thank *you*. The kids appreciate your generous donation.'

'See you,' he said. Husky, low.

Goose-bumps prickled her skin. Yeah, he'd seen her private striptease, no doubt about it.

He ducked his head as he unfolded himself and climbed out. A man in overalls, the gardener or hired help of some sort, poked his head around the side of the house, waved and disappeared back to whatever menial task he'd been assigned.

This place proclaimed more wealth, status and power than she'd see in her lifetime. A timely reminder of why Melanie wouldn't be seeing Luke bare-chested, bronzed and beautiful in firelight again.

Luke didn't look back as he headed up the path. He heard Melanie's car putter down the street and shook his head. Then stopped by the fountain and stared at his parents' house, its ornate woodwork and shutters gleaming in the wintry sun.

The house where he'd made love with Melanie. His already hardened body heated and he shifted inside his still-damp trousers to ease the pinch.

As he let himself in he smelled the familiar old waxed wood and slightly musty odour he'd never noticed until he'd been away. He went straight to the study and switched on the computer.

He wasn't staying in this house any longer than he could

help it. Not with memories of Melanie in every room, on every surface. An apartment of his own made sense—a sound investment whichever path he decided on—and he'd have his privacy.

CHAPTER SIX

'I HAVE something to tell you.' Melanie kept her voice casual as she folded the last of the baby clothes Carissa had been airing. She carefully tucked them into the cute little chest of drawers before turning to her sister.

Carissa didn't look up. Melanie doubted she heard. Eight months pregnant, she was engrossed in the tiny stitches on the cot quilt she was trying to sew. Even squinty-eyed as she carefully manipulated the fabric, she looked a picture of domestic bliss. A woman in love, about to have a baby.

Everything Melanie wasn't and didn't have. *Didn't want*. That was what she'd told herself over and over for the past few years. But her words rang hollow, clawing at her heart, and a lump rose to her throat as she watched.

'What do you think—the lemon or the lilac?' Carissa held up a couple of patches.

'Lilac,' Mel said automatically.

'For once I agree with you.' That settled, humming along to her favourite Chopin CD playing softly in the background, Carissa aligned the fabric and tied a knot in her thread.

'Carrie.' She drew in a steadying breath. 'We need to talk.'

'What? Sorry.' Carissa looked up, then frowned. Instantly contrite, she set her sewing aside, turned off the portable stereo she took with her wherever she went in her belief that the music soothed the tiny life inside her.

Melanie, on the other hand, could have done with one of

Ben's big bad bass tracks right now. Something to blow the cobwebs away.

'What is it, Mel?'

'Luke's back.'

Two little words that changed everything. Even if it was too late for them, Luke's arrival, his intrusion into her life, meant that a life she'd rebuilt piece by piece over the past few years had suddenly come unglued. And last night…

Carissa's blue-eyed gaze turned dark with concern. 'How do you know? Have you seen him?'

Oh, yeah. 'I've seen him.' A huskiness crept into her voice. 'Quite a bit of him, actually.' Her mind seemed to insist on re-hashing that first morning in her bedroom.

Carissa frowned. 'What do you mean by that?'

She explained—the Adam connection, how he'd stayed the night.

'In *your* bed? Oh, Mel, I'm sorry.' Steepling her hands beneath her chin, she studied Melanie a moment. 'I *am* sorry, aren't I?'

'I don't know.' Melanie picked up a couple of patches, put them down, then plonked herself on the floor at Carissa's feet. 'He's still the most gorgeous hunk of man I ever laid eyes on. And he looks at me—like he used to.'

'Well…' Carissa's brows puckered in thought. 'I suppose that's good…isn't it?'

'Same answer—I don't know. The overnight guest who won your getaway house?' Melanie nodded as Carissa's eyes widened. 'He came alone. Wouldn't let me drive back in the storm. At least it gave us time to talk.'

Carissa leaned over, reached for Melanie's hand. 'Did you tell him?' she asked, so softly that Melanie's eyes filled with tears.

She dashed them away, but inside she cried with long-held anguish. She couldn't tell him now, not when they'd just met up again. Some time soon, she thought, but not yet.

Melanie shook her head, but she couldn't meet Carissa's

eyes. Too much pain in the room. A pregnant woman shouldn't be thinking sad thoughts. Her own negative vibes could be bad for Carissa and the baby. 'I'm sorry, I shouldn't've—'

'It's okay; tell me what you're thinking.'

'I'm thinking he might have taken me to Queensland with him if I hadn't opened my big mouth and got in first.' Her voice fell to a whisper. 'I'll never know if he'd have chosen me over the other women in his life. The woman his parents approved of. If he was telling the truth. It was just supposed to be…fun.' And fun had cost her, big time.

'What about your letter—did you ask him about it?'

'He never got it.'

Carissa squeezed the hand she held. 'At least you know now, after all this time. You can move on from there.'

Move on? Luke might not know about the letter, but now she had other questions. Had his parents opened it to check its contents before forwarding it? Had it gone missing in transit? Melanie had no way of knowing.

'Apart from the hunk factor, is he still the same guy you remember?' Carissa asked.

Melanie's mind spun back to this morning, on the sofa. Almost without thought, she licked her lips, remembering his scent, his taste. The sparks. 'Well, his mouth hasn't lost its skill.'

'He *kissed* you?'

'How do you know I wasn't talking about his conversational skills?' Mel muttered as Carissa abruptly released her hand and—not so abruptly—pushed out of her chair.

'This calls for serious coffee and cake. I know,' she said with a wave as she headed to the newly renovated kitchen. 'Coffee for you, juice for me.'

A few moments later Mel poured the liquid refreshments while Carissa cut the fresh-baked lamington bar Ben had dropped off earlier in the day.

'So talk,' Carissa said, licking chocolate icing off her fingers as she sank onto a kitchen chair.

Her sister might be acting the casual hostess, but Melanie knew Carissa was dead serious, prepared to browbeat if necessary. And she'd learned this tactic from Melanie herself.

Melanie forked up a mouthful of lamington, chewed. Carissa's eyes didn't leave hers. 'I've moved on with my life,' Melanie said finally. 'I have work. Long hours, exhausting hours. I don't have time for an intense relationship.' And anything with Luke would be intense. Overwhelming. All-consuming. 'He might go back overseas, take up something somewhere else. What's the point?'

'And he might not. The point is, whether he's here for a day or a year, you have a history together, Mel. An unfinished history. You need to write an end to it. Don't rush into anything with him again before you figure out what you're going to do,' Carissa said.

Meaning The Kiss. The kiss that had wiped her mind of everything except how much she'd missed it. 'You think something like a simple little kiss is rushing it?'

'No.' Carissa tapped a finger on the table, her eyes steady and strong on hers. 'But I suspect it wasn't anything like simple. Or little either.'

'Hah, look who's talking—Miss Spontaneity herself.' And Ms Perceptive too.

'Only because you put the idea in my head.' A sentimental smile curved Carissa's lips, and Mel knew Carrie was remembering her first sexual adventure, which had resulted in her current state of wedded bliss.

'No, I ain't rushing,' Melanie assured her. 'I'm staying right away until I've gotten used to the idea that I'm going to be crossing paths with him in the foreseeable future—being Adam's friend's makes that a distinct probability.'

'That'll be a change for our life-of-the-party-working-her-way-through-men-like-a-box-of-chocolates gal.'

'Nothing's changed. I love chocolates. Specially the hard ones.' Deliberately she brightened her voice and forced a smile. 'But that's one dark and tempting I'll be avoiding.'

Melanie took great pains to hide the fact that her relationships stopped at the bedroom door. For the first time she considered that perhaps she was trying to hide the reality from herself.

Carissa's eyes turned serious again. 'Not for ever, though. There's always the possibility he'll find out, perhaps before you're prepared to tell him.'

'Got plans for the evening?' Adam's voice on the other end of the phone was a welcome distraction.

'Hey, Adam.' Pushing back from his father's desk, Luke rubbed the bridge of his nose. He'd tallied so many numbers today his eyes were crossing. 'No. What do you have in mind?'

'There's a poker game tonight. One of the regulars is down with the flu, we need another player. Eight p.m. Interested?'

'Sure.' He paused as a possible complication occurred to him. *Melanie*. 'Your place?'

'Is that a problem?'

'No.' But he felt the spike of anticipation drill through his body. He'd kept himself busy inspecting apartments for the past few days, not allowing himself to think about Melanie. Naked in the firelight. Her healing hands. The taste of that one and only kiss—a mistake on his part.

But whether she was home or not wasn't going to influence his decision. 'Count me in.'

Melanie had managed slow for a week. One long calorie-laden week of asking herself, 'What the hell am I doing?' Worse 'What the hell is *he* doing?'

Her roster meant she hadn't seen much of Adam, thank God—no easy way to explain she'd had a relationship with his friend and not betray how she felt: bewildered. In limbo. Alive. Confused.

Before Melanie reached her front door she could hear the sound of male voices inside. Adam's monthly poker game with his workmates, she remembered with a sigh. And last month she'd promised to make her hot chocolate sauce over ice-cream dessert in return for Adam doing her share of the chores last weekend.

So much for curling up in bed with a book after work.

She pulled her face into some semblance of a smile as she turned her key in the lock and pushed the door open. 'Hi.'

Four faces turned with a chorus of, 'Hi, Mel.'

One voice echoed in her ears, one pair of eyes lingered. A deep voice that seemed to eat her up inside, hungry eyes that lingered far too long.

Her smile remained in place but her pulse leapt. *Get used to it. You're going to see him in your apartment. No big deal.* Except that on more than one occasion she'd made her hot chocolate sauce with Luke, and, well... 'Luke.' She firmed her voice. 'How are you?'

'Fine.' He picked up a card, slotted it into his poker hand. 'How was your day?'

'Busy. Adam, about the sau—'

'Melanie, if you're thinking of backing out, forget it. A deal's a deal.' He winked at the guys. 'Didn't you admire the way I polished the bath for you? You said it felt like—'

'Okay.' She almost snapped. Dropping her coat on the couch, she headed for the kitchen. She didn't want four guys imagining her slipping into the bath. Not even one. Especially not one.

Five minutes later Melanie had her ingredients assembled, but her mind wasn't on the task. 'Make a paste with cocoa and boiling water,' she chanted to focus herself. 'Add butter...'

She knew the moment Luke stood at the kitchen door. The sensation coasted up her spine and lingered on her neck. 'Come on in, it's safe.' She didn't turn around. Her brain had curdled. For goodness' sake. 'What's next?'

'The sugar and golden syrup.' His voice sounded as rich and syrupy as the words and to her dismay she found she wanted to suck the sweetness from his lips the way she used to. Instead she dumped and stirred.

'Adam sent me in for beer.' She heard the fridge open, the clink of bottles. 'I suspect it was more for the purpose of seeing you,' he said with a wry tone.

She turned. His eyes were smiling in a casual, non-threatening way and she smiled back as the tension she'd felt eased into something approaching familiarity. 'I suspect you're right. Can you get the ice cream out while you're there? This is nearly ready.' The rich and sweet chocolate aroma swirled up to fill her nostrils.

He took out the carton, set it on the table, found five bowls in the cupboard. 'Adam says you're a wizard at this dessert. He's right.'

She didn't miss the nuance in the last two words. He leaned a hip against the bench top and watched her work as if he'd never seen her make it before. As if he didn't remember how smoothly it blended with ice-cream…and skin.

'Not bad for someone who doesn't like cooking,' he said.

'I don't mind cooking for special occasions, it's the mundane routine of coming up with a different meal every day that I dislike.' She lifted the spoon, met his gaze. 'Want a taste?'

His eyes slid to her mouth and back. She felt the impact flow through her blood and pool deep inside. Too late to withdraw her offer now. He blew gently on the spoon, dipped his thumb in the chocolate. 'The cook first.' And smeared it slowly over her bottom lip.

Oh. Good. Lord. Hot and sweet. Delicious. The texture and pressure of his thumb. His eyes alive with the same rich, dark… promise? But before she could melt into the contact and absorb the flavour of his skin, he lifted his thumb to his own mouth and sampled the residue. 'Nice.'

She sucked in her chocolate-glossed lip, nodded. Did he mean the chocolate or her? She had a feeling if she tried to speak just then her words would come out garbled.

Her legs felt weak and she slumped back against the counter for support. He leaned forward. Oh, God. He was going to kiss her, she thought, her body swaying forward to meet him, her eyelids drifting to half-mast.

Her heart thumped in her chest. She was aware of her lips opening slightly, anticipating his, the sensation of his breath against her heated cheek. A moan quivered in her throat, her own breath stalled…

Then whooshed out as Adam poked his head around the door. 'When it's convenient, Luke. Some time before midnight would be appreciated.' But his voice was light with humour.

Luke didn't take his eyes off Melanie as he picked up the beer bottles and gave her a rueful half-smile. 'Better take these in.'

'Ah, Mel…' Adam appeared again, his hand curled around the door jamb, a dare-you glint in his eyes. 'Welcome-back drinks for Luke at the Park on Friday night. You coming?'

'Oh…'

'Marie and Sophie'll be there.'

She felt Adam's jab as keenly as if he'd prodded her with a hot fondue fork. Marie might be a friend but she was also a guy magnet. And Marie knew it. So did Adam.

Which was worse? Melanie wondered, looking into Luke's eyes—watching Marie make a play for him or staying home and torturing herself by imagining it?

She'd be there. 'I'll try to make it.'

'Mel, are you seeing anyone at present?' Luke said when Adam had gone.

The question, casually asked, took her breath away. 'Why do you ask?'

He shoved his hands in the back pockets of his jeans. 'Perhaps we should see if what we had still packs the same punch. Nothing serious, we both walk away…appeased, shall we say. At least it would erase the bad feeling we parted with last time.' He walked to the door but turned back to her at the last moment, his eyes darkly intense. 'Just clarifying one point however, I don't share.'

Without waiting for an answer he left her standing alone in the kitchen.

Of all the… 'Neither do I,' she muttered, but didn't know if he heard. Indignation flared inside her as she stirred.

His condition aside, though, in a way his suggestion made some sort of sense, she thought, pouring the sauce over the ice-cream. Rewriting the end, as Carissa had said.

She shook her head, unable to believe she was actually thinking of going to Luke's welcome-back do. Even worse, considering his unexpected and dangerous suggestion that they see each other again. So much for not rushing into anything.

The following day in the Sydney Tower's revolving restaurant with the city and harbour spread like jewels below, Luke and Adam talked over old times, swapping stories and discussing mutual acquaintances.

'So how's the pathologist's love life?' Luke said over his liqueur strawberries.

'Alive and well.' Adam grinned, scooping hazelnut mousse into his mouth.

'Living with Mel doesn't make it awkward?' he asked, when what he really meant was, *Have you and Mel ever hit the sheets?*

Even though he knew Luke and Mel's relationship was purely platonic *now*, the thought of his best friend and ex-lover together that way stirred up a volatile brew of jealousy and misplaced anger that he had no right to feel. Dammit.

But Adam was astute enough to read him. 'No on both counts.'

Luke nodded, took a long draught of his beer. But his relief was only partial. He stared out at the ever-changing view of high rises, the inlets and bays with their flowing curves of blue as the restaurant turned. There was a world of guys out there. 'So…does she date?'

'Yeah, but not with the same guy more than a couple of times.'

A deep hole opened up in the pit of Luke's stomach. Did that mean she went through men like a drill through sand?

'And if you're looking for anything more specific,' Adam went on, 'I can't tell you. It would be betraying a confidence, and that part of her life is none of my business.' He paused a beat, sucked on his spoon. 'We dated too, a few times.' A moment of silence followed, broken only by the hum of conversation around them and the clatter of cutlery on china. 'But she didn't let me past first base.'

Which meant…he'd *tried*. Luke had to force himself to block out the disturbing image.

'Still, we got on well without the skin-to-skin thing,' Adam continued. 'I needed a flatmate, she wanted a place. I had no idea she and you…'

'Does she ever talk about that time?'

Adam shook his head. 'Closed book.'

'She's not into thrill sports—like skydiving or bungee jumping?' He shrugged at Adam's raised brows. 'She was always into something involving speed and height and thrills.'

'Which one were you?' His grin sobered when Luke didn't smile. Or answer. 'Not that I know of,' Adam said. 'She spends time with her sister and puts in hours of voluntary work at the hospital. She has a close bond with the kids, especially the very young ones.' Adam looked thoughtful. 'She's almost obsessive. I don't know what drives that.'

'Damned if I do either.' Melanie had never been a baby person, whereas Luke loved kids. Thing was, he could see Melanie with a baby. His baby, with Melanie's black hair and grey eyes. More disturbing, he could imagine getting her that way.

He shook it off, set his empty glass down. He didn't want to dwell on something that wasn't going to happen. He didn't even know if she'd consider his suggestion that they get together again; he'd gone a little crazy when he'd tossed the idea out there, now he had to wait.

'Enough about Melanie,' he said. 'I've found the accommodation, now I need someone to help me shop.'

He almost winced at the word. Thing was, he'd never had to shop. He'd always lived in furnished apartments, went online for anything else he needed, or purchased on impulse.

Adam rose, shrugged into his jacket. 'Better get going, then. Furnishing an apartment from scratch could take a while. We'll start with the basics and move on from there.'

A bed was the first item that came to mind—and why did that particular item have to come complete with an unsettling image of Melanie wearing nothing but a smile? Luke frowned, pulled out his wallet. 'Let's go.'

CHAPTER SEVEN

AT THE Park Tavern Melanie perched on the edge of her seat with her second glass of chardonnay. Sophie and Marie had joined her and Carissa a short time ago.

'Bathroom,' Carissa said, pushing up, and barely squeezing her pregnant belly past the table. 'Do you know how many times I've emptied my bladder today?'

Melanie grinned. 'Not a clue.'

Carissa shook her head. 'Neither do I.'

Melanie watched her sister make her way towards the powder room, then her grin faded as her eyes veered towards the band and the tiny dance floor packed with couples. Usually Melanie loved dancing—anything from ballroom to jive to techno-funk. She'd even taken a belly dancing course.

Tonight wasn't one of those nights.

Not when she knew Luke would turn up at any moment. To settle the butterflies in her stomach she took a healthy gulp or three of wine and let the sensation buzz through her veins while threads of conversation drifted around her.

'Hey, Adam's here with his mates,' Sophie said suddenly, waving to a knot of guys entering the bar.

And from the sound of their laughter it would seem they'd been imbibing elsewhere well before they'd arrived. Melanie's pulse accelerated. She didn't turn. Couldn't. She didn't want to let her girlfriends see how Luke affected her.

But Marie, always first to eye off the talent, wouldn't have noticed. She smiled. 'Well, well, well! That must be the friend.

Check out that body. Yum. And tall! I wonder if the face lives up to the rest of him.'

Despite her resistance, as if pulled by strings, Melanie's head swivelled. She blinked as her eyes focused on the details. That tanned strip of neck between short dark hair and broad shoulders. The familiar blue jumper. The way his jeans hugged his firm backside.

Her body tightened, her palms sprang with damp. She held her breath as he almost disappeared from view amongst the group. All she could see was his hair and that sexy band of flesh.

'He's mine,' Marie said, slipping out of her jacket to reveal a black see-through top and red lace bra. She rubbed her hands together and licked her red glossed lips. 'I need another drink and I think I know how to get it.'

'I reckon she does,' Sophie said wistfully as Marie walked away with speedy purpose.

Something swift and hot plunged through Melanie as she watched Marie make a beeline towards the group. Towards Luke. Marie's up-front approach had always amused Melanie.

She wasn't amused now. She felt nauseous.

'Don't you want to…?' Melanie heard Carissa's voice trail off.

Or maybe she just stopped listening.

Marie tapped Adam on the arm. The group seemed to open up at the edge and swept her inside like some sort of hungry beast eager for a hot meal. Or a hot woman.

Someone laughed and she watched Luke's profile, watched the way his cheek bunched—smiling. No doubt at something Marie said, because he dipped his head as if listening to someone shorter than him. Which included most of the patrons in the room, she reminded herself. Luke Delaney stood out in a crowd.

Barely a minute later Marie was hauling him off to the dance floor. Her heart thumping, Melanie gulped the rest of her wine, then reached for what was left of Marie's discarded strawberry daiquiri. Well, of course he'd go with her. Who wouldn't go for Marie's classic beauty? Her sexy outfit that would only look cheap on Melanie, but stunning on Marie? And why couldn't she drag her eyes away?

Suddenly his head turned, eyes scanning the room.

Then he saw her.

The force of his gaze arced across the room, hitting her right between the eyes and pinning her immobile to her chair.

His smile faded. She watched his mouth move. Was he speaking to someone in particular or the group in general? Then he started towards her.

Every muscle in her body locked. She held her breath as her heart jumped into her mouth. It was like watching a tsunami approach. All that power coming towards her in one testoster-one-packed surge.

Marie said something and touched his arm but he didn't give her so much as a glance. His eyes were fixed on Melanie. A man on a mission.

And that mission was her.

If Melanie had been standing she probably would have fallen—or fled.

He didn't stop until he was an arm's length away. Until she could see the pinpricks of stubble on his chin, the faint sheen of perspiration on his upper lip as he said, 'Hi. You made it.'

There was a hint of something more in his tone, as if he was remembering the other night when he'd suggested that they explore what they'd had five years earlier.

Before he'd walked out of the kitchen without waiting for an answer.

Was he going to expect that answer tonight?

That thought jolted her out of the sensual thrall and she blinked as the tavern's sounds and people around her came into focus again. She forced her lips into a smile. 'Did you think I wouldn't?' She patted her sister's shoulder. 'You remember Carissa?'

'Yes. Hi, Carissa, good to see you again,' he said, stepping nearer, smelling of something spicy and cool, a startling counterpoint to the heat emanating from his skin.

'Hello, Luke.' Carissa's blue eyes searched Melanie's face, returned to Luke. 'Mel told me you were back.'

Luke's gaze met Melanie's as if to say, *What did you tell her?*

Ignoring it, she introduced her friend. 'And this is Sophie. Sophie Watson—Luke Delaney.'

'Hi, Sophie.'

'Hi.' Sophie's brow puckered in thought, then cleared. 'Luke Delaney. You're the guy who won the getaway. The one Melanie—'

'So you two know each other.' Marie sidled up beside Luke, giving Mel an eyebrow-lift that said, *Why didn't you tell me?* 'Why don't you join us, Luke? I'm sure we can find another chair.'

Her red lacquered nails danced over Luke's hand. The large tanned hand he'd laid on the table in front of Melanie. The one that had stroked across her bare flesh...

'Thanks, that won't be necessary.' Luke curled his other hand around Melanie's upper arm, pulling her gently but firmly to her feet. 'Excuse us,' he said to the group in general, his eyes locked on Melanie's. He leaned down so his breath stirred the hair at her temples. 'Let's dance.'

She didn't have time to look at Marie, or Carissa. A jitterbug was already doing a dance in her belly. It didn't help that he kept that proprietary hand around her arm as he led her onto the dance space and into the throng of dancers.

It definitely didn't help when the band chose a slow bluesy number as they got there.

She forgot the press of bodies as couples jostled for room. Her head spun with the wine she'd drunk and Luke's proximity, her heart throbbed in her ears, frantically out of sync with the slow beat of the music.

She curled her fingers in front of her in an effort to control the space between them, but he propelled her closer with a subtle press against her spine.

Oh, help. Her pumpkin halter-neck top allowed ample exposed flesh for his hands as they shimmied over and down her bare back.

'Your friend's a threat to mankind,' he murmured against her ear.

'Is that why you were in such a hurry to dance with me? Are you a coward, Luke Delaney?'

'I wanted an excuse to put my hands on you.'

Her pulse leapt at the intimate admission. Her own hands—where could she put her hands? On his waist, not *round*, just on. Barely. But she could still feel his body heat through his jumper, the hard muscle beneath.

He noticed her hands-off-the-merchandise thing. Smoothing her hair behind one ear, he leaned down. 'Are you a coward, Mel?' he said, echoing her own words over the mellow sound of the clarinet.

She felt his breath, the touch of his lips and the whiskey-edged voice against her earlobe and shivered as the sensation whispered over her skin and ribbon-danced through her body. But she leaned back so she could see his face, jerked her chin higher. 'I'm dancing with you, aren't I?'

He grinned, pulled her back against him and said, 'How's your week been?'

'Busy.' Slow. 'How about you?'

'Same. I've bought my own apartment. In Double Bay.'

'Double Bay?' One of the most exclusive suburbs in Sydney?

'Can't go wrong there—great views, close to the city. Outdoor entertaining area and spa.' His voice deepened. 'Huge master bedroom with a view of the harbour.'

'I didn't think you were staying that long...?' Was he?

'What gave you that idea?' he said, expression inscrutable, but for a flicker of something behind his eyes.

'Adam said...' She trailed off. 'Do you have a job here, then?'

'Not yet.' The coloured lights played over his face, a

kaleidoscope of pink and green and gold, but his eyes dared
her to dance another kind of rhythm, to take another kind of
risk. 'Put your arms around me properly.'

O...kay... Still watching him, she drew in a slow breath
and slid her arms around his back, watched his eyes darken
and loved the fact that she could still turn him on. She felt his
muscles tense as she walked her fingers up each vertebra. 'Like
this?'

'Exactly,' he murmured in that same rumbling voice.

Yes. Exactly. She gave up trying to pretend to herself that
she could resist. Her nose brushed against his jumper. Right
in that familiar little hollow below his breastbone. Where the
air mingled with the scent of fabric softener and warm, masculine skin.

It seemed like for ever since they'd danced. And so familiar
it seemed like yesterday. She settled in, turning her head so it
rested against the hard pillow of muscle. The music faded into
the background as his hands cruised down her spine, over her
hips, increasing the pressure until her breasts were flat against
his chest, her thighs pressed intimately to his.

Heat. Everywhere heat. From the top of her head where his
cheek lay, to the soles of her five-inch-stiletto-clad feet.

It took a moment to register that the music hadn't faded. It
had stopped. And they were still clinched together on the dance
floor knee to knee, breast to chest, while couples eddied past
them as they made their way back to their tables.

She reared back, away from the soft feel of his jumper, the
intimate way he was sliding his fingers over her nape beneath
her hair.

The scorching intensity of his eyes as he trailed a fingertip
across her brow and said, 'You don't have a headache, do you?'

'Why?'

'Because right now I want an excuse to take you away from
here.'

Her blood turned to syrup and pounded through her body.
It wasn't her head that was aching. She wanted to say he didn't

need an excuse, until she remembered—'Aren't you the guest of honour here tonight?'

'I'll speak to Adam. We've been drinking since five, it'll be okay. I'll tell him something came up.' His eyes sparked with devilish humour.

Melanie stifled a girlish giggle. That 'something' had been nudging her stomach for the past few moments. 'I'm with Carrie, Luke. I can't just leave her here.'

'She's not alone. I'm sure she won't mind, or we can give her a lift home first. But we'll check.'

We. Like a couple. Her pulse did a quickstep as they parted—Luke to speak to Adam, Melanie back to her table where Carissa sat with a mineral water balanced on her tummy and a peeved Marie sucked at something colourful in a tall glass. Sophie was engrossed in conversation with one of the guys at the next table.

'Carrie, Luke and I—'

Before she could couch the rest of her sentence in words suitable for company, Carissa looked over Melanie's shoulder. 'Go ahead…if that's what you want.' Meaning if that's *who* you want.

Melanie turned and saw Luke making his way across the room, tugging his leather jacket on as he walked, his hair reflecting strands of red amongst the brown, his eyes focused wholly on her.

Her whole body yearned. It wasn't wise, it wasn't smart, but she wanted. She wanted with every aching beat of her heart. She wanted to take that chance Luke had talked about and see where it led.

Carissa nodded. 'I'm having fun watching and remembering what it was like when I could slide onto a dance floor like that and gyrate with the best of them. Ben'll pick me up when I'm ready.'

'Okay.' Melanie patted Carissa's swollen tummy. 'See you all later.'

And just like that, she picked up her bag and walked out with Luke Delaney.

For the first time in years she felt the old freedom and laughed as they stepped outside into the cold night air, feeling her hair float around her face as she spun a full circle.

Live the adventure. Something she'd believed in and followed all her life. Until life had changed. Now that same itchy feeling, the thrill of it, twitched between her shoulder blades.

The old risk-taker was emerging from the stone she'd been hibernating under. She spun again, watched the stars pinwheel with her as she revelled in the joy of it. Watched the slender crescent of moon dance dizzily.

'Steady.' Luke's hands grasped her mid-spin. Solid, secure. Earth-shattering. And he was only touching her shoulders. 'You forgot this.'

He held out the coat she'd left behind and slid its silky-lined warmth over her shoulders. 'Thanks.'

He turned her around until they stood toe to toe. The car park's blue lights sharpened his features. Again she noticed time had carved deeper grooves around his eyes and mouth. He looked…more rugged.

But he was still Luke and she was feeling far too good and a little too tipsy to worry about the changes time had etched on her own body. Or to think about how those changes might affect whatever was about to happen between them.

He hadn't let her go so it was a simple matter to reach up on tiptoe and touch that rough-textured jaw. To feel it tighten beneath her fingers as he dipped his head.

She waited a moment, relishing the sharp edge of anticipation, the slow, serious burn in her veins. Then she leaned into that whisper of space between them and put her mouth to his.

Warm, firm. *Welcome home.* She'd relived that kiss from a week ago over and over. This was better; this time she'd taken the initiative and was ready. She let her mouth open to the flick of his tongue, tasted heat and desire against the flavour of beer.

Here was rightness. The way he feathered his thumbs over

her cheeks and lifted her face up for better access, the rich melding of breath and lips and tongues.

Dark as the night, the low growl in his throat rumbled, ridged velvet against her fingertips as she skimmed them over the tendons of his neck and throat. Luke was her ultimate adventure. *Take that chance.*

She pulled back to whisper, 'You can put your hands on me now,' then deepened the kiss. Her mouth tingled and warmth settled in her belly as he slid his thumbs over the drumming pulse in her neck. But not enough, not nearly enough.

Maybe the ground trembled or perhaps it was his hands as he lowered them, tracing her shoulders, calloused thumbs grazing her collar-bones. He followed the line of the silky tie that held up her halter top and down, over the sides of her breasts... then paused.

He lifted his lips a fraction and his eyes blazed, burning coals in the dimness. *No bra.*

She leaned forward so her breasts swung forward a little, into the hard cups of his palms. And sighed at the aching, tingling fullness that only intensified when his hands began to move.

Sensation stabbed through every pulse point in time with the muffled bass of a nineties party hit emanating from the tavern. He massaged her breasts in slow, erotic ever-decreasing circles till he was gently pinching her nipples.

A group of male patrons exited the building, their raucous laughs slicing through the stillness.

'Don't even think about backing off,' she warned, sensing Luke about to pull away. She grabbed Luke's hands and pressed them against her.

She wanted his hands under the fabric. She wanted to feel his mouth on her breast, to stroke his hair while he scraped and tightened his teeth over her nipple. 'I've been thinking about your suggestion,' she said, breathless.

'So have I.' His breath puffed out on the cold night air. 'I take it you've made a decision?'

She grinned. 'Come on.' Grabbing his hand, she headed for the secluded garden at the front of the building next door, laughing at the delicious idea taking shape in her mind.

She found a patch of lawn by a row of bare poplars, thin white ghosts in the dark. The air was a fresher green here away from the oil-slicked car park. The moon sprinkled silver on the dew, splashed shadows beneath the bushes. Quiet, not quite private.

Standing beside Melanie, Luke ran his knuckles down the side of her face, staring at the grass with a dubious expression. 'Are you thinking what I think you're thinking?'

They were metres from the road. It was undoubtedly illegal, slightly dangerous, definitely adventurous. She turned into his embrace, clapped her hands on his cold cheeks. 'Why not?'

He huffed out a half-laugh. 'Isn't it a trifle chilly?'

'We'll make our own heat. Here…' She had to touch him, to feel his whiskery skin against her fingertips, the softer, warmer skin between neck and shoulder where his pulse beat strong and not quite steady.

'And here…' Breathing in the smell of leather and wool, she crept her hands inside his jacket, spread it wide.

'And—' she heard the huskiness in her own voice as she reached between his thighs '—here.' The hard ridge of masculinity was its own blast furnace. Molten steel. 'No risk of frostbite,' she murmured and ran her fingers along his length, remembering how it felt flesh to flesh. Mouth to flesh.

He inhaled sharply. She tossed her jacket on the grass and watched the jumble of emotions cross his face. Then she moved in, wound her arms around his neck and tugged. He followed her down with a groan, positioning himself as a shield against any passers-by. She snuggled back against her jacket, felt the wet grass beneath her calves, felt it seep through her skirt.

His expression was one of total absorption as he fumbled with the tie behind her neck, turning to smouldering desire when he finally freed it.

'You're still the most beautiful woman I ever laid eyes on,' he murmured, drawing the ties toward him.

And how many women had he laid eyes on since her to make that comparison? Right now it didn't matter as his lips and hands followed every inch he bared as he slid the fabric slowly down her torso. He lingered over the skin between breast and shoulder, even longer when he found her nipples, cherry-dark in the moonlight.

She revelled in the contrast of cold air, hot hands and hotter mouth as he rubbed and nipped and suckled. Squirmed in an effort to get more. To get nearer. Her hands roamed over his chest and up under his jumper to feel hot, masculine flesh and the up-tempo beat of his heart.

With little encouragement from her his hand slid lower, his palm scorching a trail over her thighs as he pushed up the hem of her dress. 'Mel…' His chest heaved, his sharp exhalations sounded like a freight train. 'Are you still on the Pill?' he rasped.

'No.' Her breathless word was swallowed by his mouth as he planted a firm kiss on her lips.

'That's okay.' He pulled something out of his pocket and fumbled with his trousers.

She held her breath. Any moment now he was going to slip inside her. He was going to take care of the pulsing need gathering force low in her belly. Her fingers dug into the hard flesh of his shoulder. He was going to take her to that magical place only he could.

They were going to make love.

The moment shattered as the realization—and the implication—seeped through her mind and her hand flattened against his chest.

Reality stomped all over the romantic interlude. A crushing pain filled the space that moments ago had bloomed with bright promise. She barely noticed her moisture-slick nipples rapidly chill in the cold air as she pushed at him.

Wake up! This isn't the young geological engineer you fell in lust with—the one you told yourself was no ties, just fun.

Just sex.

Hadn't she learnt anything from that experience? That actions had consequences? The last time they'd been together, they'd done more than make love.

They'd made a baby.

CHAPTER EIGHT

'MEL?' Luke's hand stilled on her thigh, his voice thick with restrained desire, his breathing ragged. 'I thought you wanted this. Did I get it wrong?'

'No, but I'm sorry, I can't.' *I want to, but I can't; it brings back memories I thought I'd gotten over.*

Blowing out a heartfelt sigh that echoed her own sentiments, he touched her cheek with a gentle finger. 'It's okay, Mel. It was a mistake—this place. I should've taken better care of you.'

He pulled her top up over her still-tingling breasts and knotted it behind her neck. Took her trembling hand and helped her up. Grabbing her coat, he shook it once, then pulled it around her shoulders.

She couldn't look at him and see the heat in his eyes turn cold, to acknowledge the confusion she knew she'd read there, so she pulled out of Luke's arms when he would have held her closer. Hugged her coat tighter against the chill that had suddenly grown icy. The worst part, the part that scraped every nerve in her body raw, was that Luke didn't know why.

Without thought she half ran, half stumbled across the grass. Away from his proximity, his potency. She only knew she needed to put distance between them. From the relative safety of the footpath she looked back to see his eyes narrowed at her and a furrow between his brows. The thump of bass from inside the tavern seemed to echo inside her skull and was giving her the headache Luke had mentioned a few moments earlier.

This thing between them was a lot more scary and a lot more complicated than she'd imagined.

Luke let her go. He needed a few moments anyway to get his raging hormones under some sort of control. If he'd planned better he wouldn't be standing here with a fire in his groin and the only woman who could put it out clicking her heels a cold, long-distance stare away.

Damned if he knew what that plan was.

He huffed out another long breath that left a trail of vapour on the air as he crossed the car park towards her. *Slow. Easy.* If they were going to have any sort of relationship he'd have to tread carefully. Right now it was as fragile as fuse wire.

'Hey,' he murmured when he reached her. The air crackled with the same tension that snapped in his veins. Her eyes were glazed and over-bright, her lips drawn tight.

'I…I'm sorry.' She rubbed at the dampness on the arms of her coat. 'It was a stupid idea—I forgot it's winter. Last time we… Last time it was January.'

Which gave him no hint about what she was really thinking. 'It should be me apologising.' He stroked a hand over her hair, hating the fact that something had chased away the vibrant spontaneity she'd shown him a few moments ago. Her taste remained hot and potent on his tongue; the scent of her lingered in his nostrils.

But any chance of taking what they'd started tonight to the next logical step vanished quicker than a lump of coal down a mine shaft.

'Is it something I did? Something I can help you with?'

She shook her head, the shadowy depths of her eyes flickered in the stark lighting. 'My problem, I'll deal with it. I just want to go home.'

'I'll take you.' He steered her towards a taxi outside the pub. Her fingers felt cold and fragile in his as they climbed into the cab. The atmosphere remained chilled and formal as they drove back to her apartment. His groin tightened as all the scenarios of how the evening might have ended burned through his brain.

In her bed. Her on top, her ebony hair brushing his chest, his thighs. Those magic healing fingers working over his muscles. And then sliding into her warm, wet centre as she arched that amazing body over him, her moans as she came, squeezing him dry. Begging for more.

One glance at the rigid posture of the woman beside him, the knotted fists on her lap, the way she preferred the passing scenery to looking at him, put that notion to rest.

But more worrying than the knowledge that he wasn't getting naked with Melanie tonight was the change he'd witnessed in her. For a few precious moments she'd been the Melanie he knew. Then it was as if she'd flicked a switch. Damn, damn, damn. What the hell had happened?

At her door it kicked him in the gut to see clouds in the depths of those grey eyes as she stepped back inside and told him, 'I'm not good company right now. I think it's best if you leave.'

'Okay.' But he laid his palm against the door when she would have closed it. 'We've still got it, Mel, tonight proved that. Whether you want to explore it some more is up to you.'

Melanie sagged against the door and waited until she heard the cab leave. Her headache was marching up on her, throbbing in time with her pulse. A migraine. And a reminder, a red flag warning her that any involvement with Luke had consequences.

Her breath sighed out and tears prickled the backs of her eyes. What would Luke have done if he'd known she was pregnant? She'd asked herself that question many times over the years. She asked herself again now. She didn't know if he liked kids.

Frowning, she hissed out a breath between her teeth as pain sledgehammered her temples. She thought she knew him, what he did and didn't like. His interests and idiosyncrasies. But she didn't know the most important thing of all: she didn't know if he liked kids. Because it was the one thing she'd never been game enough to explore. They had been temporary lovers; kids hadn't come into the picture.

Pushing away from the door, she moved quietly through the empty apartment using the light filtering through the open curtains to guide her to her room. She closed her door, switched on her lamp and adjusted it to low.

From the back of her wardrobe she drew out her mother's old jewellery box. She didn't look often these days; over the years she'd learnt to accept her loss as one of life's turning points, but with Luke's scent on her skin, his voice still in her ears, she felt the need to look now.

The wooden box, inlaid with mother-of-pearl, was wrapped in a silk scarf and one of the few items she'd kept as a reminder of her mum. The familiar scent of her perfume still lingered inside the box as she opened it.

Inside was the stuff of her life. Her own hospital ID tag from when she was born. A child's gold charm bracelet. Her ticket to her favourite rock band's concert.

She withdrew the photo of her first ultra-sound. The grainy black and white image was all she had left of that tiny life. She traced the delicate outline with a fingernail. She'd never had the chance to feel it grow inside her, to count fingers and toes and know the sound of its cry.

'If your father had known about you...'

Would it have made a difference? Luke might never have taken that job in Queensland. Never fulfilled his dreams of becoming a successful engineering geologist. Instead he might be working for his father, a situation she now knew wouldn't sit well with Luke.

Resentment and bitterness would have followed. At least now he'd become his own person. 'I never wanted to trap you, Luke.'

Her eyes lingered a moment before she set the photo where it belonged—in her memory box—rewrapped the silk and put the box back in its place.

They'd been lovers for three months. Hardly time to build a solid and trusting relationship. She hadn't known she was pregnant when they'd parted. She hadn't known an upset stomach could nullify the Pill's protection.

But she'd wanted to tell him, to give him the opportunity to be a part of his child's life, even if he'd had no desire to be a part of Melanie's. That hadn't worked out. Then she'd had the miscarriage in her second trimester. Over the years it had grown easier to let go of the loss, to look forward, to build a new life. On her own. She'd carved a career for herself through sheer stubborn will and damn hard determination. But she'd never, ever forgotten.

Just as she'd never forgotten how deep her feelings had been for the father of her baby.

Before he left again, she owed it to Luke to tell him.

Melanie went off duty at eleven p.m. after a fourteen-hour stint. In addition to her own little patients who were all sleeping soundly, she'd helped out in Emergency with a spate of accident victims, one asthma attack and a suspected appendicitis. If she stayed any longer she was likely to do more harm than good.

At least she could take a bath and crawl into bed and sleep without the dreams that had kept her awake for the past how long? Since Luke had walked back into her life. He was detrimental to her well-being, a definite health hazard.

In the two days since she'd seen him, she'd worked hard, taking extra shifts to block out the images of Luke. He hadn't called—he'd left it up to her.

She missed him.

Which only proved it would be a mistake to get involved again. She'd end up being hurt when he left, just like the last time.

The hospital doors whooshed shut behind her as she stepped outside, wrapping her purple sheepskin jacket tight over the uniform she hadn't bothered to change out of.

She was in a mood; she was drop-dead tired. But the extra

hours she'd put in had done nothing to wipe the sensual images of Luke's hands on her flesh, the wet tug of his lips at her
breast, the incredible way her heart had hammered as they'd
moved to the band's slow beat.

She increased her pace, wishing her soft work shoes made
a more satisfying noise on the concrete as she crossed the car
park. Unlocking her car, she tossed her bag on the seat and
turned the key. Nothing. She laid her head on the steering
wheel. She wanted to cry.

A frustrating hour of waiting later, the auto service told her
the car needed towing—better still she needed to buy a new
one; this heap was dead.

When she finally arrived home in a cab, she found Adam
and—she groaned at the bad timing—Luke in the living room
watching M*A*S*H reruns. Ignoring Luke's, 'Hi' and the sudden blip in her heart rate at the sound of his voice, she concentrated on steering herself towards her room.

A light hand touched her shoulder. 'Whoa, slow down a moment. What's wrong? You look knackered.'

'I've been at the hospital for fifteen hours, my car's dead
and I will be too if I don't get some sleep,' she said, and kept
walking.

'Good idea, Mel,' she heard Adam say. 'Let yourself out,
mate, when you're ready to go,' he told Luke.

'No, it's okay...' Melanie waved a hand in her sensitive flatmate's direction. 'Don't vacate the room on my account, I'm
just passing through.' Adam had never done so before when
she'd had male friends over—why tonight? Or was it a prior
arrangement between the two guys?

'Thanks for the company,' Luke said as Adam picked up the
bowl of popcorn and took himself off to his room.

Luke's hand gently squeezed the nape of her neck, stopping her mid-stride. He turned her to face him. 'You need to
sit down and unwind a bit first, have a warm drink.'

'I don't think so...' She trailed off under the sensual on-
slaught. He was undoing the pins that held her heavy plait to

her head, relieving the tension her tightly wound hair always caused. Oh, yes. Pleasure sighed through her as he released its weight, unravelling it with gentle fingers, massaging her temples.

'We'll sort out your car tomorrow.'

'I told you it's dead. Nothing to sort out.'

'Good old Maurie's given up on it, eh?'

'Mikey,' she corrected, but he already knew that, didn't he? 'He's not on call twenty-four seven. I rang the auto service. They towed it away.'

He brushed his mouth across hers, once, twice. Not demanding, not expecting, just a soothing balm to her over-stressed body.

Her knees sagged; her shoulders slumped. She closed her eyes and felt the last of her mood fall away. She was quite literally dissolving in his hands.

All that remained was an overwhelming fatigue that bordered on pain. She was beyond caring whether he stayed the night or not, as long as she could sleep.

'You want that warm drink?' Luke murmured against her mouth. 'Or do you want to go straight to bed?'

Her pulse spiked. *What?*

But he just shook his head. 'I meant alone, Mel. You look dead on your feet.'

'Chamomile tea,' she said as she stepped away. 'Too many coffees today. Third tin from the right. I'm going to have a bath.'

She clarified the 'bed' situation in her own mind while she turned on the taps and dumped in bubble bath. She *wasn't* going to make love with Luke, but *if* she did she was going to be awake enough to enjoy it. Did that make sense?

Probably not. A sign that her brain was in meltdown. And he hadn't even mentioned making love. She gathered her hair into a large clip on top of her head, then stripped off her uniform, let it drop where she stood and slipped into the waiting bath's soothing embrace. Let her aching head rest on the padded towel and drifted...

'Mel? Mel!' Luke's voice seemed to come from a long way off.

'Huh?' Her eyes fluttered open. Straight away she noticed the water had lost most of its warmth. Her cooling skin was a sharp contrast to the hot, dark eyes that met hers. But overlying the heat she saw concern. 'What...?' She made an uncoordinated attempt to sit up, splashing water over his white T-shirt, then gave up and lay back.

'You make a habit of falling asleep in the bath?' His worried tone changed to gruff. Thick and turned on.

'I wasn't asleep.' She looked down at herself. The bubbles were all but gone, leaving her naked and wet and thoroughly exposed. Dear God.

'I waited, I called. Take it from me, honey, you were asleep. Here,' he muttered, and held out a towel.

She noticed he kept his gaze pinned to her face. Colour slashed his cheek-bones, she saw his Adam's apple bob as he swallowed. She had to swallow herself once, before she attempted to lever herself up.

Immediately she was enveloped in terry towelling. 'What time is it?' she asked, gripping the edges of the towel together, her teeth chattering as she stood on the bathmat.

'A little after one. You need to get dried off.'

Before she could coordinate her limbs to perform the task herself he began rubbing her back through the towel. She almost purred like a cat as his knuckles worked over her spine.

Then with a rough-throated sound he took the edges of the towel in his hands and slid it from her body. He dabbed at her face, her shoulders. The simple task became slow, hot, sensual. Residual steam sheened his skin, clung to the hairs on his forearms as he wiped her throat, along her collar-bones.

'I can do...' She trailed off, unable to finish her sentence.

He paused, the towel bunched in his fists against her décolletage, watching her with barely restrained desire in his chocolate eyes. She knew he saw the flare of her response because they heated, darkened. He dropped to one knee in front of her.

Slowly, a gentle torture, he dragged the towel lower, abrading skin that turned exquisitely responsive. Every tuft of cotton was a pinprick of pleasure as he massaged her breasts. Her nipples tingled and tightened, sending ribbons of sensation spiralling to her core.

Her head rolled back, her arms dropped to his shoulders. Helpless, she stood while her pulse hammered in her ears, beat through her veins, throbbed in that place between her thighs where she burned with need.

His breath feathered over her breasts and abdomen. Knowing he was inches from her bare skin brought a renewed flare of response.

She felt the towel leave her body. He lifted her right foot, placed it on his jeans-clad knee and dried each toe, then her calf. Repeated the procedure with the other foot. She arched her instep against the gentle coercion and moaned her enjoyment.

But it wasn't only the hot lick of anticipation, the knowledge that she'd waited five years for this feeling again. It was Luke. The man she judged every other man against. His gentleness, his thoughtfulness. His patience.

She let her feet spread wider on the bathmat. The cotton chafed the back of her knees, and up, along the insides of her thighs. A rough caress, a sparkle of fire. She felt him pause again and looked down to meet his eyes. Intense and blazingly aroused. She tightened her fingers on his shoulders and kept her gaze locked with his.

The chafing resumed, his knuckles searing her skin as he worked higher, rubbing in long, slow passes until the fabric—and the slippery glide of one long finger—touched her woman's flesh. Her throat felt clogged in the clammy confines of the room; her legs were trembling.

'Luke.' His name spilled from her lips, but it was all she

could say. She was on that knife point, that razor's edge, poised for flight.

He stopped his ministrations and she almost whimpered. 'You okay?' His voice was hoarse and his eyes were glazed.

'Yeah.'

One slow rasp of the towel and her climax spun her over that edge. The room faded to white, the floor tilted and she collapsed into Luke's arms.

A few shallow breaths later she thought she might be able to speak. 'I think I'm dry now. Mostly,' she murmured.

He chuckled, but it sounded strained. 'Let's get you into bed, honey. You need sleep.'

She felt his muscles tighten as he rose and carried her to the bedroom. He didn't turn on the light and she got a dim glimpse of him as he pulled down the covers and laid her on her bed.

She shivered. The sheets felt like ice against her overheated body. 'Cold,' she murmured.

'Okay.' She heard Luke close the door then felt the bed dip as he slid in beside her fully dressed. He pulled her against him so they were spooned together, her back instantly warm against his T-shirt, her bare legs against thick denim. Her bottom against the thick, hard and unmistakable ridge of his erection.

Lethargy stole through her body like a thief, robbing her of her chance to roll over and tug down that zipper digging into her spine. For the first time in five years she didn't feel quite so alone in the world. As she fell asleep it slid through her mind that it was dangerous. She could get used to that feeling.

CHAPTER NINE

WHEN Melanie surfaced from the best sleep she'd had in a long time full daylight flooded her room. She stretched lazily and snuggled backwards. When she didn't encounter a hard, warm body she rolled over and found the space where Luke had been cold and empty.

She told herself she *wasn't* disappointed, but after last night… She blocked out the images and reined in her run-ahead thoughts. *Don't get used to it, just enjoy it while it lasts.*

Grabbing her tracksuit, she dressed and padded to the kitchen. The cup of chamomile tea Luke had made for her last night still sat on the table.

She brewed coffee while she thought about him and why he'd been here when she had come home. Had he come with the intention of seeing her or to catch up with Adam? Probably the latter since she'd swapped shifts when a colleague had called in sick at the last minute and Luke couldn't have known.

Which was just fine, she told herself. Then she noticed the string of numbers scrawled in pen on the inside of her wrist. His mobile number. Her skin tightened. One of their old pastimes had involved writing messages on each other's bodies. In all kinds of interesting places. She rushed back to her bedroom and stripped off, shivering in the cool morning air.

There, on the upper swell of her left breast. The Double Bay address of his new apartment. Heat flowed through her at the thought that he'd pulled back the covers and written on her bare flesh. That he'd looked at her naked while she'd slept on in blissful ignorance. One wasted opportunity to enjoy the sensation of his eyes on her body.

She redressed, made her way to the living room, picked up the phone and started punching in the number he'd given her, then stopped. Did he expect her to call and thank him? Just because he'd given her an incredible, mind-blowing, earth-tilting orgasm?

Oh, God. She had to sit down. She had to lean her arm on the table while she poured her coffee.

And nearly scalded herself when the phone rang. It was Luke.

'You're awake. How did you sleep?'

'Probably a lot better than you,' she said, and heard the grin in his gruff laugh.

'Did you get the address?'

'Yes.' She rubbed at the spot on her breast. 'I got it.'

'Go to your front door.'

'What?'

'Just do it.'

'Okay, I'm there.'

'Now open it.'

She shielded her eyes with a hand as the sun's full glare bounced off a white Holden Astra in the driveway. Crêpe-paper streamers on the antenna snapped in the breeze.

An involuntary gasp left her lungs. He hadn't. He wouldn't... But he had.

He got out when he saw her, grinning like a kid at a birthday party, and dangled the car keys from a finger. She squinted, looking closer. The keys were on her pewter daisy key ring.

Very carefully, she set her coffee on the floor by the door. 'What have you done?'

'Bought you a car. It's got air-con and—' he leaned inside '—registration papers, new tyres—'

'You shouldn't have.' A sharp pain centred in her chest. She sounded ungrateful. She didn't want his generosity.

'Why not?' His grin melted away and the pain in her chest

doubled. 'You needed a damn car. I was helping a friend out, that's all.'

Why not? Because a gift like that came with strings. Hadn't he stipulated no strings? Sex was one thing, a new car was something else. She shook her head. 'I don't need your help. I've been doing okay by myself.'

She marched back inside on trembling legs, sank onto a kitchen chair, cradled her head in her arms on the table. His idea of helping a friend out was a world away from hers. With his wealth, it probably wasn't such a big deal. And it didn't have to come with strings; she wouldn't let it.

Her anger dissipated enough to turn around and walk straight outside again. 'Luke, I'm s…' She trailed off when she saw she was talking to the wind.

Guilt thundering through her veins, she flew down the steps and out onto the footpath in time to see his tail-lights burning as he turned at the intersection.

Her brain in a whirl and not knowing what to do next, she hurried to the car. He'd left her keys in the ignition. A street directory was open at the Double Bay address on the passenger seat. 'Think of everything, don't you?' she muttered, snatching it up.

But even if she left now she couldn't catch him. She wasn't familiar with the car or Double Bay. Locking the vehicle, she took her impatience inside. Okay, she needed to calm down and dress and figure out how to take back some control.

Five minutes later she pulled on her cherry-red cowl-neck jumper and skinny jeans. At the last moment she shrugged into her sheepskin jacket and stuffed her nearest available scarf in her bag. Grabbing the directory, she hurried down the steps, shook her head in disbelief again when she saw the car gleaming in the sun.

She slid behind the wheel and sat a moment. Wow. She ran a hand over the dashboard. Clear windscreen and almost-new car smell. And just a whiff of Luke's aftershave to get her hormones in an uproar again.

Should she send him a text message to tell him she was on her way? No. An apology should be face-to-face.

Forty-five minutes later Mel parked behind a classy-looking Mercedes and stared up at the luxury apartment. One of two, state-of-the-art, huge balconies with floor-to-ceiling windows and views to die for.

Another tree-lined street that reminded her of his parents' home. Her hand tightened on the steering wheel. She so didn't fit in.

A cold wind with a faint tang of the sea snapped through the front of her loose-weave jumper and tugged at her hair as she climbed out. She hugged the edges of her sheepskin coat together, hyper aware of its ragged appearance as an immaculately groomed woman came out of the architectural monstrosity next door, eying her curiously.

Removing her sunglasses, Melanie returned the look, then smiled. Just because she didn't belong, didn't mean she lacked basic courtesy. Mrs Perfect smiled back before slipping into the Merc and driving away.

Now there was nothing for it but to walk up those stairs. All twenty or more of them. She tucked her sunglasses in her bag along with the house-warming gift she'd bought Luke on the way, slung it over her shoulder and carefully locked the car. Fiddled with the toggles on her coat.

Listened to the rapid thump of her heart in her ears telling her to turn around and go home. The man who lived in this luxury wasn't the man she'd known.

But he'd been that familiar man with her last night. The thump in her ears escalated. And that familiar man hadn't lost his touch.

The word was a catalyst for the sudden tingle in her nipples, the gush of heat between her thighs as she remembered the sensation of crisp towel against her flesh and the slick warmth of his finger as he'd slid it inside…

Sucking in a breath of cold air, she forced herself to concentrate on now. *Now* she was going to climb those steps and knock on that fancy stained-glass door, hand him the keys and say her apologies.

Luke swiped a towel over his face and watched Melanie from his bedroom window. There she was, the object of his frustration—and anger, dammit—standing at the bottom of his steps looking as if she might bolt at the least opportunity. Except for the lifted chin.

In her trademark hotch-potch of colours she was a splash of summer sunshine in the middle of winter. Then he frowned. 'Damn independent woman,' he muttered, with a last dab over his freshly showered body.

Grabbing his jeans, he dragged them on as he padded through his apartment. He reached the front door as the bell chimed.

He opened it, then stepped away abruptly, not wanting to smell her rose and vanilla scent that wafted in on the breeze. Not wanting the reminder of how her skin had smelled last night as she slept had beside him, how soft and smooth it had felt beneath his hands. Along the front of his thighs. Against his aching erection.

She stood on the doorstep, knuckles white from gripping her jacket and making no attempt to step inside. Her defiant chin lowered as her eyes slid to his bare chest and remained there for so long he swore he could feel every hair spring to attention. Not to mention other neglected body parts.

She noticed too—he could tell by the stain of pink high on her cheeks. But she stayed where she was, on the other side of the door, and met his gaze. 'I want to apologise.'

He thought he saw a softness flicker in her eyes but it was gone before he could blink. 'I was rude,' she continued, withdrawing a brown cardboard box from her bag and thrusting it at him. 'And ungrateful.'

'Agreed.' But he accepted the box, then reached out and tucked her flyaway hair behind her ear.

The contact seemed to confuse her, it sure as heck confused him. Then he realised they were both angry, but somehow they both knew where the other was coming from. 'What's this?' he asked, turning the box over in his hands.

'A house-warming gift.'

He looked up, into her eyes. 'Only accepted if you accept mine.'

'There's a big difference between a simple gift from the local shops and a car. I'm used to being on my own, Luke, and making my own decisions.' She looked away, at the harbour, and he sensed she was thinking of something sad. Then she seemed to shake it off and turned back to him, her grey eyes wide and focused on his as she said softly, 'Can I come in?'

With a nod, he moved back to allow her entry.

His whole body tensed as she stepped inside and closed the door. Blame it on one long and frustrating night, but he fought the iron grip of desire, the urge to back her up against the door and plough into her until the sounds of their pleasure rang from the rooftop. He glanced up at the lofty ceiling. That was a whole heck of a lot of pleasure.

'What?' She followed his eyes as she set her bag on the floor.

'Thought I heard voices,' he muttered. He blew out a breath. 'Come on in. Below-floor heating,' he said as he led her across the wide expanse of carpet. 'Sofas are due tomorrow. They didn't have the colour I wanted in stock. The rest is pretty much in order.'

He aborted the tour of his bedroom at the last moment, opting instead for the kitchen.

'Open your gift,' she said, sitting down at the table.

He thumbed open the brown cardboard box. Inside were two plain champagne flutes and a wood-topped corkscrew. 'Thanks, Mel.' Simple, inexpensive, but it meant a lot that she'd thought to buy it.

'I know, you probably have a whole stack of glassware. Great views,' she said, immediately changing the topic, turning away again, the remnant tension from last night humming in the air

'You can never have too many glasses.' She was trying to ignore that tension and he needed a caffeine jolt to take the edge off. 'Want coffee? I was just about to make some. Or would you like to christen the glasses with something stronger?'

'Coffee's fine. Mind if I explore some more?' She waved a hand and was already walking away.

'Go ahead.' It would give him time to cool down.

'Oh, by the way, I hope you're free this afternoon,' she called over her shoulder. 'I owe you one.'

Oh, yeah. Frustration gnawed low in his belly. But he didn't think that was what she was referring to. Grinding his teeth, he turned his attention to coffee-making but his mind was fixed on where he suspected Melanie was now—in his bedroom.

He could picture her admiring the harbour view, then turning to admire the king-size bed. Or was it vice-versa? He remembered his unmade bed, sheets crumpled from his restless nights. He imagined his sheets crumpled from a different kind of restlessness. Melanie's pale skin shimmering against his midnight-blue sheets, her hands moving over the linen. Over him.

He clenched his teeth as he poured water over coffee beans and stupidly hoped what Mel had planned involved crowds and adrenaline.

'Okay, Luke,' she said, over her mug a short time later. 'I've got a whole two days off. You wanted not serious. I'm suggesting not serious.' She had that familiar gleam in her eyes that he'd learned to associate with things that usually involved either risk or daring or both.

'What do you have in mind?' he ventured. And guessed adrenaline was definitely on the agenda. He'd been too hasty in his hopes for what she'd dreamed up, he thought, with a sense of trepidation.

'Luna Park. Fairy floss, a couple of rides…' That gleam turned positively wicked.

Luke's stomach did that queasy jiggle it always did at the mention of that place.

'Who chooses the rides?' He heard the uneasy tone of his own voice.

'I do.' She sipped her coffee, seemed to consider. 'Maybe I'll let you choose one, if you're nice.'

Hardly mattered. If Mel let him choose all the rides but one, he'd still know that this afternoon was going to be a roller-coaster ride in more ways than one. He could only be grateful he hadn't suggested an early lunch. 'Anything else?'

'Yeah. We'll come back here after and eat. I'll even let you cook.'

'Generous of you.' Luke blew out a breath. If he could face food. He pushed back his chair, already sweating a line of nerves down his spine. 'Let's get it over with, then.'

Luke had avoided theme parks since he and Mel had been together, and not only because the sight of fair-goers being flung into the sky turned his stomach to mush. He couldn't get past the image of them together whenever he got a whiff of the warm metallic smell of greased machinery and hot doughnuts.

As they strolled through the familiar gaping mouth at Luna Park's entrance the past returned in a kaleidoscope of sights and sounds. He won her a teddy at one stall, a green velour snake at another. They rode the Ferris wheel and a couple of low-grade thriller rides, all within sight of the Harbour Bridge.

The white-knuckle ride Mel chose that had had his gut churning with dread in anticipation wasn't the one he'd disgraced himself on five years ago, but it wasn't much better.

'You're not going to chicken out on me, are you?' Mel said—a statement, not a question—as he watched a pale-faced teenager barely walking away unaided.

'No way,' he muttered.

But it took a good half-hour before the clammy sweat dried and he could face the fairy floss Mel insisted was part of the whole experience.

They stayed until evening darkened the sky to purple and

Sydney twinkled with thousands of lights reflecting on the inky harbour.

Until the feel of Mel's hand in his was no longer enough. He wanted those hands on more than his mouth as she fed him pieces of her doughnut. He wanted those eyes now dancing with pleasure, sobering and darkening with passion.

'We've seen enough,' he said, tugging her away from the merry-go-round's tinkling music. 'Time to go home and eat.'

But by the time they reached the car Luke had one objective in mind and it wasn't eating.

'Ooh, the luxury,' Mel sighed, settling herself into the passenger seat as they left the car park and turned into the traffic.

He swore he heard the sound as she ran a hand over the butter-soft seats. As if she was wondering how they'd feel against her bare skin.

He gripped the steering wheel as a sudden vision of a naked Melanie draped across the seat rolled in front of his eyes. Her bottom sliding over the supple leather as he pulled her closer. Her eyes, hot as molten steel as he reached between her silky smooth thighs, spreading them wider, finding her wet, slippery heat...

With a wry shake of his head he picked up speed as he crossed the coat-hanger bridge. Any more X-rated images like that and he'd be forced to pull over and turn them into a reality.

'What's wrong?' Mel said and he felt those eyes staring at him. 'You in pain...or something?'

'Forget it.' He cleared the huskiness from his throat.

'No. What were you thinking? I want to know if we're on the same wavelength.'

She touched his knee, just a friendly pat, but he felt the subtle tightening of her fingers and the instant tensing of his thigh muscles. 'No questions.' He swore beneath his breath as he slowed for a truck that cut in front of him.

'You're hard as a—'

'No talk.' He almost snapped. He took one hand off the

steering wheel to cover hers, eased it off his thigh and set it on her own. 'Not if you want to make it home in one piece.'

Was that a purr? he wondered as she snuggled down in her seat. From the corner of his eye he saw her undo the toggles of her jacket. She raised a hand to her pony-tail, tugged off the band and dragged her fingers through her hair with a sigh of satisfaction.

Damn, he'd wanted to do that. He inhaled the scent of her shampoo as she moved, the subtle drift of the soap she'd used last night.

Last night. When he'd found her in the bath. His blood turned thick at the memory. Anticipation grabbed him hard between his thighs.

He shifted, his discomfort growing to epic proportions as he navigated the roads on virtual autopilot. He was reacting like a randy adolescent, thinking like a horny teenager.

Making up for lost time, he thought. He'd never been an average kid. 'No son of mine plays with dirt,' his father had told him when Luke had shown an early interest in geology.

Nor had he been an average teen. To the loud jeers of his mates, he'd preferred cataloguing his rock collection and his safe geological field trips to dating the up-market daughters of his father's acquaintances. Thank God he'd seen the error of his ways when he'd reached his twenties.

He glanced in the rear-view mirror and sneered at his reflection. Still nothing like the free-spirited Melanie who dived into life without a reserve parachute.

The Roll-A-Door rose with a barely audible rumble and security lights winked on as he pulled into the driveway and up the steep incline into the undercover carport. He turned off the ignition. In the silence he could hear his own heartbeat thundering in his chest, Melanie's soft breathing.

He turned to look at her. Her hair draped her shoulders like a scarf of black silk and he had to reach out and touch. Smooth and cool against his fingers. Then the lights went out, leaving them in total blackness, and the silence deepened with dark velvet promise. Leaving his hand on her hair, he edged closer. His forehead bumped something bony.

'Ouch,' she said with a jerk.

'Sorry.' He lifted a hand and discovered he'd bumped her nose. His fingers drifted lower, over lips compressed into a thin line—of pain or annoyance or both. His lips followed his fingers, then his tongue, skimming her mouth until it softened. Then he felt her pull away with an impatient swish of fabric over leather.

'Let's get out of here.' Her sharp response made it clear she wasn't impressed with their surroundings.

And why would she be, with a perfectly good bed a few metres away? He grabbed his keys. 'Right with you.'

But he hesitated a moment before climbing out. Was his plan to keep things between them casual flawed? Would he be able to walk away when they decided they'd had enough? More likely she'd be the one to walk first. Some other guy would take her fleeting fancy.

Hold that thought. It made it easier to keep everything in perspective.

CHAPTER TEN

THE LIGHTS came on again as they made their way to a connecting door and entered the apartment. He tossed his keys on the kitchen table. He wanted nothing more than to grab her hand and keep walking till they hit carpet—forget the bed.

But his duty as host demanded he grit his teeth against the tightness in his jeans and ask, 'You want to eat?'

'Maybe.'

Her ambiguous answer had him turning. Maybe? Had he been misreading those sexual innuendoes in her eyes? Against the floor-to-ceiling windows, framed by the city and harbour lights she looked like a model posing for one of those Come Visit Sydney posters. That had to be an encouraging sign, right?

His whole body burned as she shrugged off her purple fleece, revealing a glimpse of red strap beneath her jumper in the process, and let it fall where she stood.

'First I need to get out of these tight boots,' she said, tugging them off. 'My feet are killing me.'

He empathised. Tight seemed to be the order of the moment. But he wasn't looking at her feet. His attention was wholly focused on her lips. Glossy with oil from the sugared doughnuts they'd shared. A few clear granules still clung to the corner of her mouth. 'You have sugar on your mouth.'

'I do?'

She raised a hand to brush it away but he captured it in his own as he nudged her backwards towards the living area. He continued to hold her, rubbing his thumb over the pulse in her wrist, feeling the thump against the tender skin, the firm mounds of her breasts as he leaned in. 'You do.'

Her lips parted slightly as he dipped his head, flicking out his tongue to sample that sweetness. And, God, it was sweet, dissolving on his tongue as he licked his way from one corner, over her bottom lip to the other. When she opened her mouth to speak—to moan? to gasp?—he slipped right in to savour the next course.

But she pulled back slightly, and he watched her eyes at half-mast in the reflected light from the kitchen. Beneath the heavy lids he recognised the same burning intensity he knew she'd see in his. But something else flickered in those depths.

Was he moving too quickly? Or not quick enough? Damn it all, what had happened to the sunny girl he'd spent the afternoon with?

More than anything at this moment he wanted to erase that look and calm whatever-the-hell doubts had put those clouds there. A sudden urgency gripped him. *Don't give her time to think.* He reached out, pulled her back, hard against his body. 'Melanie.'

Her name sounded like wine on his lips. Smooth and sultry and seductive. With something perilously close to desperation, he rushed his hands beneath her clothing, finding slinky satin and firm flesh. Heard the same desperation in her shallow breathing as her body tightened.

He had her jumper up and over her head before he could say 'finesse'—not how he'd wanted it to be, but helpless against a sudden fear that something might keep her from him as it had the last time. A fleeting image of lacy red bra crossed his vision before he unsnapped it, tossed it away.

He caught a handful of her hair in his fist, pulled her head back until her gaze locked with his. Shock, heat and desire darkened her eyes. 'There's only us,' he rasped, his voice thick, his hand abrading her scalp. Unable to think beyond this moment.

'I—'

'Only us. Now. Here.'

'Only us,' she whispered, and he heard the tremble in her rough-edged voice.

He tightened his hand against her head, drawing her tight against him with his other hand at the small of her back so that she was arched against him.

'Only us. Right. Now.' Her hot, breathy demand feathered across his chin, her hands wasting no time diving under his jumper and up to tweak his nipples into hypersensitive bundles of nerve endings. 'Now, now, now.'

The pulse of his blood beat through his veins in time with her chant, an insistent drumming that spread through his body, hammered in his groin as he fumbled with the top button of her jeans.

Shoving the denim over her hips and thighs with her panties, he palmed the tight, hot skin of her buttocks. The manoeuvre wasn't smooth, it wasn't skilled, but in a tiny corner of his still-functioning mind he knew she didn't want that any more than he. Somehow he peeled off his jumper, tossed it away.

When she overbalanced he compensated and they slid to the carpet together in a tangle of limbs and heavy breathing. 'You okay?' He pushed up on his elbows.

And was seized by a primitive possessiveness at what he saw. Her skin glimmering pale and pearlescent in the glow from the kitchen. Glossy black hair, mussed from his hands, flowing across the floor like an ebony lake, her cherry-dark nipples puckered and erect.

She arched her back against the carpet, her legs shifting restlessly. 'I will be. Soon.'

'Soon.' He pushed her thighs apart and knelt between them. Just where he wanted her. Where he'd dreamed of having her—awaiting his touch, her woman's flesh waxed and naked and glistening with arousal.

His breath stalled in his chest. How many times had he woken rock-hard and sweating with this image burning behind his eyeballs, the taste of her sex hot on his tongue, her scent filling his head? 'You're all I remember and more.'

There was an instant of absolute stillness, as if he stood with her on the rim of a volcano about to erupt. But only an instant. Then molten pewter eyes met his, his skin blistered with their heat and ignited, and he was hurtling towards that precipice.

Melanie surrendered to the longing snaking through her body and gave herself up to the moment. The heated carpet felt abrasive against her bare back, the backs of her legs, Luke's hands hard and uncompromising on her thighs as he pushed them wider.

Her exposed flesh quivered beneath his gaze. Every pore tightened, every beat of her pulse echoed through her body. She was remembering too—every sexual encounter of their short relationship flashed through her mind.

How he could turn her inside out with one look from those hot toffee eyes, one glide of his finger over wet, slippery skin.

How they'd turned each other inside out, again and again. Sex with Luke had always been a sunburst of fierce and frenzied energy. And flying too close to the sun…

But he gave her no time to ponder the past. Leaning down, he blew a stream of warm air over that tight, trembling woman's flesh. So light yet so potent; she felt herself splintering like fragile glass, shattering helplessly beneath his gaze. She cried out, something mindless as he blew again and sent her spinning to climax.

'You're amazing, you know that?' he said, watching her as she opened her eyes to look down her body at him. Still watching her, he slid down between her thighs. Passion blazed in his eyes, turning them dark toffee. Then his tongue plunged into her, a wicked, delicious torture to her still-spasming body, his fingers digging into her flesh as he clenched her hips to hold her still.

'Luke…' She clutched at his hair, his jaw, to centre herself, to drag him up and over her. Felt the slide of firm muscles and hairy masculine skin, then his hands on her breasts, tweaking her throbbing nipples into shamelessly jutting points.

Hard, hot denim chafed her lower body. Abruptly, she

reached between them, flicked the stud of his jeans undone, diving her hands beneath the elastic of his briefs to find him hot, damp, hard as steel.

His stomach muscles tightened under her hands and he muttered something harsh, his breath shuddering out against her mouth.

She darted her tongue out to soothe the tight line of his mouth and tasted her passion on him. 'I've got it,' she told him when he would have lowered his hands to his waistband. 'You just keep doing what you're doing.'

The sound of the zipper being wrenched down elicited a groan that brought a similar response to her own throat. Her pulse danced impatiently. 'Hurry.'

'Doing my best,' he muttered, shoving the offending garments down. Reaching into the pocket of his jeans to grab a foil packet from his wallet, rip it open with his teeth and sheath himself. He tossed the foil packet over his shoulder.

She froze. They'd never used a condom—she'd been on the Pill to regulate her cycle. What if he made her pregnant again? Ben had used a condom and Carissa had been caught—it wasn't fail-safe. Could she go through that alone again? The answer was no.

He must have seen the doubts in her eyes, felt her pulling away. He smoothed a hand over her cheek. 'It's okay, Mel. Whatever you're thinking, don't.' His hand slid around to gently squeeze her neck. 'I need you tonight. I've wanted to do this to you since that first day in your bedroom.'

And then they were both naked and skin to skin and pregnancy was only a distant warning in a far corner of her mind. She needed this, needed him, more than she'd realised. And he needed her.

That flood of need engulfed them both, sweeping them along in a torrent of dark heat and battering sensations. When he plunged deep inside her she arched up to meet him. Renewed desire geysered up, almost drowning her in a tide of love.

No! Some distant corner of her brain registered that emotion and instantly discarded it. It had never been about love. It had been about lust, needs, wants.

Luke must have felt her flutter of denial because he slowed his pace momentarily to reach up and smooth her damp hair from her brow. 'Stay with me.'

'I'm right here.'

Keeping her eyes focused on his, she matched him, stroke for stroke, faster, faster, until reason vanished and thought was impossible and there was only the primal drive to completion. Mind dim, she gasped at the glory of her release as he emptied himself inside her.

Hours later Melanie woke slowly to the unfamiliar warmth of another body beside her, Luke's slow, even breathing ruffling the hair at her temples. She opened her eyes to watch him sleep. Relaxed, like a god satisfied he'd performed his divine duties.

Her body echoed that sentiment in a dozen different ways as she stretched muscles that hadn't been used in a long time on his luxurious satin sheets. Hmm. *A dozen different ways.* Not quite, she thought with a sated smile, but they'd get round to it.

Last night they'd snacked on whatever they could find in the fridge, then come to bed and made hot and furious love again. In the early hours of the morning Luke had woken her and they'd had slow, sleepy sex, drifting back to sleep still joined.

And she was feeling entirely too good to think about why this might be a mistake, to consider the consequences of a relationship with Luke. No. Not a relationship. This was about sex—great sex—the best ever, but anything else—

'Good morning.'

She turned at his gravelly voice and found him watching her through barely raised eyelids. 'Yes.' Her fingers crept up to his chest to toy with a pebbly male nipple and she saw his eyes widen. Darken. 'It is. A very good morning.' Cocooned beneath his quilt, surrounded by the scent of last night's passion.

'Mmm.' He covered her fingers with his, guided them over his chest in lazy circles. 'Do I get a kiss?'

'Depends—' she wiggled closer, slid her leg over the hard, hairy length of his, noting another hard length nudging her thigh '—on what you're offering for breakfast.'

'What did you have in mind?'

She could tell by the sultry look he cast her that he was offering himself as part of the menu and pressed an open-mouthed kiss on his sleep-dry lips. 'Nuh uh.' Another kiss in the warm, musky hollow of his neck. 'I need sustenance before we go another round. Coffee—freshly percolated, strawberries...and hot sticky buns.'

He blinked. 'How about two out of three?'

'Hmm.' She trailed her lips over his shoulder, nibbled an earlobe. 'I'll make you a deal. I'll put on the coffee and prepare the strawberries if you'll go get the buns. I saw a mini-supermarket yesterday not far from here with a Sweet Delights bakery.'

A pained expression crossed his face. 'You sure you want to eat first?'

'Oh, yeah.' How far was Luke willing to go for her? Buying a car was simple for him. Dragging himself away from a warm bed and a naked woman and into a windy winter's morning to fetch sweet treats—

'Is this some kind of test?'

For answer she arched across him, rubbing her sex-slippery flesh along the ridge of hard hip-bone, turning herself on in the process. 'Call it a bribe.'

'Some would say that's illegal.' Quick as a whip for someone who'd just woken up, his hand shot down between her legs. 'You still want sticky buns first?' He dipped a finger into her centre, plunged deep, then withdrew, dragging it over her swollen centre.

'Yes...' The word exhaled on a sigh and sounded damn unconvincing.

Two fingers. Three. Plunge then withdraw, oh-so-slowly,

making lazy circles and creating a warm, wet friction that promised faithfully to take her to paradise—

'Sugar-cinnamon or icing?'

Her thighs fell apart and she arched into his hand. 'Su...gar— Oh...you...don't...play...fair.'

'Okay. I admit it, that was unfair.' He took his hand away and threw back the quilt. A wash of cool air doused her exquisitely aroused body, peppering it with goose-bumps.

He was grinning, the cad, as he bent to tug a nipple between his teeth. It was only a marginal satisfaction to see that he was as aroused as she.

'I think I'll walk,' he said with a smirk, reaching for his jeans. 'Get some exercise.'

'Coffee'll be cold if you do.' She tugged the quilt back under her chin and glared at him. 'And so will I. Careful with that zipper.' She winced as he dragged it up. Tight fit.

He grinned again as he took a T-shirt from a drawer. 'Very well, you win. Okay if I take your car? It's right out front.'

She nodded. 'Keys are in my bag on the table.'

'Right. See you soon.'

'Very soon.'

When she heard the front door close she sat up, swung her legs over the bed. Took three deep breaths and ordered herself to put her arousal on temporary hold. Make coffee.

She'd left her clothes where she'd stripped them in the dining room—rather, where Luke had stripped them—so she inspected Luke's wardrobe and found a thick flannel shirt to put on.

The floor was warm as she made her way to the kitchen, the apartment cosy. She found coffee beans and switched the percolator on, then began stacking plates into the new dishwasher.

Luke arrived back as the coffee finished percolating. He set an aromatic box of buns on the table and pocketed his mobile phone. She reached for mugs, turned and began pouring. 'Just in time.'

'For what?' he said, his voice layered with meaning. He came up behind her, and slid his hands over the front of the shirt, rubbing her nipples into tight peaks on the way down. 'Mmm. You smell good.'

'I'm wearing *your* shirt,' she pointed out.

'Hmm. I smell good, then.'

He rucked up the shirt from behind and she gyrated her bare bottom against his denim-covered erection. The sensation of bare ass and denim was a stunning turn-on she hadn't expected. She tossed him a sexy glance over her shoulder. 'Sticky buns later?'

He didn't reply as she'd expected. 'I just listened to my messages.' He tightened his arms around her, locking his hands over her navel and nestling his chin on her shoulder. 'Mum and Dad got back last night. They wanted to know why my phone was switched off.'

Melanie's hands tightened on the coffee-pot, but she kept her voice light. 'What did you tell them?'

'That I was tied up with a naked woman all night and she wouldn't let me use the phone.' He gave her a light-hearted peck on the cheek. 'I'm meeting them for brunch in an hour.'

She stirred sugar into Luke's coffee, concentrating on hiding a disappointment she had no right to feel, then stepped away to set the mugs on the table. They hadn't seen their son in a long time; who was she to resent it? She *didn't* resent it. Much. 'So, I guess you're kicking me out, then?'

'No. No,' he said again, as if considering his words. 'It's just that they'll probably want to come over at some point and see the apartment...'

'And you don't want me here.' Nor did she want to be here. She smiled, but it felt as brittle as glass. 'That's fine, Luke. I don't particularly want to be caught bare-assed by your parents.'

'Hey.' He followed her to the table, finger-combed her hair from her face. 'I'm sorry it's this morning, of all mornings.'

Melanie was too. They could have been snuggled up in bed,

feasting on hot and sticky and it wouldn't have been only the buns. Which only made her hyper-aware of Luke's scent on her skin, the slight rasping soreness between her legs from their night together.

But it was morning. Their night was over. 'It's okay, I need some down-time and I wanted to catch up on some sleep and some washing anyway. You need to see your parents, Luke. I understand. Really,' she assured him, seeing the doubts in his eyes.

'Stay for coffee and cake first,' he said, his hands still in her hair.

'Thanks, but no, thanks.' The sweet smell of cinnamon didn't sit at all well with the lead balloon in her stomach.

'After all the trouble I went to?' He tugged on a hank of hair, again with that light-hearted manner.

Obviously he didn't even consider introducing her to his family. Nor did she want to come face-to-face with his father after what he'd done.

'I'm sure you'll want to tidy the apartment before you go—' *make the bed, air the room, dispose of the condom packet: make that packets* '—so I'll just be on my way as soon as I'm dressed.'

Face it, Melanie. This was what having a no-strings, sexual relationship was all about:

You don't get involved with your partner's family.
Your partner's family always comes before you.

CHAPTER ELEVEN

THE moment his parents were out the door Luke snatched up his phone and punched in Mel's number. A quick call to let her know he'd been thinking of her.

He'd spent most of the day catching up. He'd met them at their home, taken them out for a light meal, shown them over his new apartment. Talked business, kept any thoughts of the business opportunity he'd been offered to himself.

But he hadn't been able to get Melanie and what they'd shared last night out of his mind. Hadn't been able to rid himself of the image of the warm and willing woman in his bed this morning and the sweet promise of more. The cool woman a scant hour later as she'd walked down the steps and driven away.

'Come on,' he muttered and had to force himself to unclench his teeth. She was disappointed they hadn't finished what they'd started, that was all. And she wasn't the only one.

Finally. But it was her answering machine that picked up. Something unfamiliar and strangely deep knifed through him at hearing the simple sound of her voice on the line. He wished he could see her. Smell her, touch her, tell her... what? 'It's Luke, Melanie. I hope you'll be awake when I get there—I'm coming over,' he said, and disconnected.

Damn. He ran both hands through his hair and stared through the window. What was happening to him? One night of hot sex and... He shook his head. Sex. That was all it was.

Wasn't it? Sex with a woman who'd been in his blood for five years.

A short time later he leaned on the doorbell with one hand, a bunch of wind-tossed irises and daffodils in the other.

The two-tone chime echoed inside but no sounds of movement were forthcoming. Adam wasn't home—he'd already checked the car park—but Melanie's new car was parked in her parking space.

'I know you're in there, Melanie.' He raised his voice. 'Open up or I'll be forced to use the key Adam gave me.' A lie, but it had the desired effect. He heard a door shut, saw a blur of colour through the frosted-glass panel.

The door opened a fraction. He took in the pale skin and dark circles beneath her eyes—a lack of sleep? Or was there something more hiding behind that carefully neutral expression?

'Can I come in?' When she inched open the door further he stepped inside and closed it quietly.

'Adam didn't give you a key.' Her crossed arms drew attention to her pushed-up breasts. Red flannelette barely covered her bottom, giving him a view of long, shapely legs. Legs that had been wrapped tight around him last night. His body still burned with the memory.

'Adam doesn't give any of his guy friends a key without discussing it with me first,' she said. 'It's a rule we have.'

Luke nodded, holding out the bouquet and searching her eyes. 'Very wise. I'm sorry about this morning.'

'I understand.'

No, she didn't, because she took the flowers avoiding his fingers, avoiding eye contact.

'They're beautiful. Thanks. I guess you've been busy,' she said as he followed her to the kitchen while she hunted up a vase.

'Yeah.' He'd rather have been exploring her hidden and not-so-hidden places all over again. No, that wasn't quite true, he admitted to himself. He'd also wanted to know why she'd gone so cool. He wanted to understand her.

She gave him an almost-smile, but it didn't reach those eyes, which still didn't quite meet his. 'I guess it could have been worse. They might have turned up at the apartment without ringing first.' Amazing how that tiny lift at the corners of her mouth could transform her whole face. Like the sun coming out from behind storm clouds.

Also amazing, he thought as he watched her wrench on the tap and fill the vase with water, how quickly the sun could disappear. He was suddenly desperate for even a glimpse of that brilliance once more.

'Sorry.' She nodded at laundry strewn over every available surface. 'The clothes dryer's broken. The living room's a bit of a jumble sale at the moment.' He hadn't noticed the room smelled of soap powder and take-away until she pointed it out; he'd been too preoccupied with the scent of her freshly soaped skin.

She cleared a space on the coffee-table and set the vase down, rotated it. 'I've been meaning to get the darn thing repaired, but—'

'Forget the washing. And the flowers.' He slid his hands around her waist and pulled her close, breathing her in, enjoying the way she felt against him. 'I want to talk to you.'

'I don't want to talk.'

He smiled at her muffled words against his chest and kissed the top of her head. 'Neither do I.'

'I want to sleep. We didn't get much last night.'

'I thought that's what you were doing?'

'No. I've been running errands, doing washing.'

'Well, we can go to bed now, if you want.'

'Alone, Luke.'

His buoyancy deflated, but all wasn't lost, she wanted him— he could tell by the way her nipples pressed against him, the way her hips angled against him as her legs pressed against his. 'I'll go. In a little while.'

The knowledge that she was naked beneath that red sleep shirt had his blood rushing to his groin. He couldn't resist smoothing a hand over the tempting swell of her breast. Coaxing a nipple into a hard little peak.

'Stop...' But she moaned and arched her breast into his hand.

'You don't want me to stop.' He dipped his head to suck at her nipple through the flannel. Let his hand roam over tempting curves and valleys and down, until he found the hem of her shirt. 'I don't want to stop either.' He walked her backwards until her thighs bumped the couch.

She stroked a hand down his chest and over his belt buckle. Drawing a thin line with one exquisitely potent fingernail over the straining zipper in his jeans. 'It always comes down to sex with us, doesn't it?'

Something tingled through his veins. He stared at her for a few unsteady heartbeats, trying to gauge her mood. He thought he saw something flicker in her eyes, cool and flint-hard beneath the warm glow of arousal.

He covered the hand poised over his zipper and flattened it against him, feeling the heat of her palm burn through his jeans. So tempting to unzip and let those expert fingers take care of his need. But suddenly taking care of physical need wasn't his priority right now. He wanted to know more about the deeper emotions he'd witnessed. Reluctantly he removed her hand. 'Mel...'

'Luke...'

They both spoke at the same time.

'You first,' he said.

The serious tone, the hesitant way she said his name, had him bracing himself. She pressed a hand to her belly as if in pain and he could've sworn she was going to say something, but she let out a sigh that seemed to come from the depths of her soul and closed her eyes. 'It's nothing. You were going to say...?'

She was closing him out and he didn't like the feeling. 'Remember last night?' he said. 'When I touched you all over, with my hands—' he let a finger caress the side of her cheek '—my lips' kissing her springtime-smelling hair '—my tongue…' He swept the hair aside to nuzzle the soft skin between shoulder and neck and laved a slow path to her earlobe. 'I lost myself inside you and you lost yourself with me.'

And that was what he'd missed with the other women he'd slept with. The way she gave herself to him, honestly and openly and without inhibition. It was more than sex.

It was…more.

The sudden revelation detonated inside him, deep in his core and radiated out to the tips of his fingers.

'I haven't forgotten.' She turned her head a little, baring more of her neck and giving him greater access. 'You're my rose-cream-smothered-in-dark-chocolate man.'

He couldn't say why that description disappointed him. It had all the right ingredients, but the word 'man' sounded suspiciously temporary. As if he was good until hard-caramel man came along.

Temporary. That suited him fine, right? For someone who'd lived and loved 'temporary' all his life? And she'd been the one who'd said their relationship was never going to be permanent.

Five years ago he'd figured her words had just bruised his ego, but right now they damn near drew blood.

Last night had meant something to him.

And while he was trying to come up with what that elusive 'something' was, she opened her eyes and looked at him. Looked at him as if she could see inside him.

He looked back, searching for answers. 'Have you ever wondered what sort of relationship we might have if there was no sex involved?'

She blinked, long lashes framing her eyes, which looked too large and too dark against her pale skin. 'No sex?' She shook her head. 'Our relationship's based on sex. That's what it is.'

Was she right—was sex the only attraction? Did she believe that? Because he wasn't so sure that skin to skin was enough any more. He was tired of living alone, he wanted someone to come home to, someone to share life with at the end of a long day. He'd wanted that for a long time. He just hadn't realised it till now.

'Go home, Luke. Your family comes first, go and get re-acquainted with your parents again. I'm on night duty for the next few days and the Rainbow Road committee's meeting to discuss our next fund-raising project. And I promised to help with—'

'Why do you push yourself so hard?' Almost as if she was trying to leave herself no free time. Or was she only trying to leave no time for him?

'I've been doing it for the past five years—it keeps me focused.'

No, it keeps her distracted, he thought, remembering the girl he'd known who'd played the occasional hooky from work to play with him. She was using work to shut out whatever her problem was.

Her rejection, and the fact that she hadn't opened up to him, disturbed and irritated him and he stepped away. He couldn't suppress the tension in his fingers as they curled into fists against his sides, nor the tightness in his voice when he said, 'Fine. Go and have your sleep.'

Without a backwards glance he let himself out. But he stood on her doorstep for several moments watching the winter sun sink slowly behind the shadowed apartment buildings, feeling the chill of the wind slice through his shirt.

What had happened in the past few years that had changed her?

'Let Ben do it.' Carissa's hand waylaid Melanie as she rose to help him clear the table.

'But he cooked, it's only fair…'

'You've got to work tonight and Ben loves washing dishes.' She batted her eyelashes at him and smiled sweetly. 'Don't you, my love?'

Ben skirted the table with an armload of dirty crockery to give Carissa a kiss. 'You forget we have a dishwasher.'

'I didn't forget, but you're not going to put my eighteen-carat-gold-rimmed china in the dishwasher, are you?' she stated firmly.

'Wouldn't think of it.' He swapped a conspiratorial grin with Melanie and disappeared into the kitchen.

Carissa hauled her very pregnant form out of the chair. 'Excuse me a moment…'

A moment—no, Melanie checked her watch—several moments later, she was still waiting. She finished off her half-glass of wine, her limit for a working night. She could hear the two of them talking in the kitchen.

The talking ceased for a bit, then she heard Carissa laugh—or more precisely, giggle. And a very masculine, very turned-on groan.

Melanie squirmed on the polished mahogany chair. Since Luke's return into her life her libido had sprung out of hibernation and hit the ground running. Thank God she'd been working the night shift. She'd punished her body by doubling her daily jog and had fallen into bed exhausted.

Another giggle drifted on the air, cut off abruptly, as if someone, or something, had stifled it. Like a mouth.

Picking up her glass, she marched to the kitchen and glared in mock annoyance at the clinched pair. They were in lock-down mode, hard up against the dishwasher, with Carissa's T-shirt pushed up and her bare stomach between them.

Lost in each other. The phrase echoed in her head. That was what Luke had said about the two of them the other night. Deliberately blocking the memory, she cleared her throat. 'Ben, you'll give that baby palpitations. Go find something else to do, I'll finish up here. You've monopolised your wife quite enough, it's my turn.'

'Sorry, Mel.' He grinned at her, rubbing circles over Carissa's belly. 'Got a little carried away.'

'Go,' a thoroughly kissed Carissa ordered and pointed the

way to his studio. 'I told you she'd find out your dirty little secret.' She turned to Mel, her face flushed, eyes shining. 'He's
developed a fetish for pregnant women's bellies.'

He lifted his hands and backed off. 'Okay, I'm gone.'

'I sincerely hope that's singular, as in "woman".' But Melanie
already knew that without a doubt. 'How is my little niece or
nephew doing in there?' She crossed the floor and put her own
hands on Carissa's belly.

A sense of wonder filled her, and tonight she also felt the
familiar keen sense of loss. The baby kicked against her hands
at that moment; she looked up and met Carissa's eyes.

'Mel…' Further words were unnecessary. The dulcet strains
of Ben's guitar floated through the closed door to the studio,
a poignant piece that seemed to echo the moment.

'It's okay, Carrie. I'm okay. And I'm so happy for you and
Ben.'

Carissa nodded, placing her hands over Mel's. 'I can't believe it's happening again so soon.' She straightened up, arch-
ing backwards and pulling her T-shirt down at the same time.
'Let's go back into the lounge.'

'But these dishes—'

'Can wait. Ben'll do them when you've gone.' She snagged
Melanie's arm on her way and brightened her tone. 'I want an
update on your love life. All the gory details. I remember when
it used to be you asking me. What's been happening?' She
plonked herself on the sofa and patted the space beside her.

Melanie couldn't sit. She wandered to the window and
looked out into the darkness. Then told her sister about the
night she'd spent with Luke and the arrival of his parents.

'I nearly told Luke about the baby, Carrie, when he came
by after, but I couldn't. I don't even know how long this thing
between us will last this time. Or if there is an "us".'

Carissa snorted. 'You couldn't have been paying attention to
the way he was looking at you in the pub that night. Everyone
else noticed.'

The words made her heart do a funny little tap-tap, but she

said, 'What's the point of—' she nearly said 'falling in love' '—a relationship if he goes overseas and I never see him again?'

'Did he tell you that?'

Melanie shook her head. 'It's just a gut feeling.'

'You could go with him.'

'If he asked me like he did last time?'

'He bought an apartment,' Carissa pointed out.

Melanie shrugged. 'An investment.'

'Okay, leaving all that aside, how do you feel about him now?'

Mad, passionate, head-over-heels. Crazy. 'The same. And different—I look at him and see the man I loved. The man who fathered my baby.' She heaved a sigh. 'The only man I'd ever want to father my baby.'

'The man who doesn't know,' Carissa said softly.

'I tried telling him five years ago but it didn't happen. What good's it going to do now?'

'That's a cop-out, Mel. And it's not being fair to him. I know because I thought the same thing about Ben. Figured he'd be better off. If he finds out for himself…'

'Not likely—I don't keep contact with the crowd from those days.' But Melanie sighed, knowing Carissa was right. Knowing she'd tell him. *Not* knowing the consequences.

He'd made it clear what he thought of their relationship. She couldn't allow herself to fall in love…or was it already too late?

Luke was caught up with his parents for the next few days. He resisted the urge to call Melanie. He wanted to surprise her and he wanted to do it right. A call to Adam gave him the information he needed. Tonight she got off at nine p.m. and she wouldn't be on duty till three p.m. the following day. A simple supper, then.

Candlelight. He set the squat jasmine-scented candles on the polished wooden table. Women went for candles. And nice crockery. He'd had a devil of a time picking out the china. He frowned at the two settings. Had he thought simple? He almost laughed. He couldn't see himself eating off the dainty rose-sprigged plates, but he'd bought a set anyway, putting his black octagonal back in the cupboard. The new silverware gleamed; the crystal flutes sparkled.

He'd hired a chef to cook the supper—Vietnamese spring rolls with dipping sauce, a salad plate of cucumber, bean sprouts, spring onions and coriander. Caramelised pineapple and citrus fruits with spiced Muscat cream to follow. All chilling in the new stainless-steel refrigerator.

He checked the time, and with a last satisfied glance over the arrangements, he grabbed his keys.

'What are you doing here?' Melanie came to a halt on the hospital's linoleum floor, her heart fluttering at the sight of the man she least expected to see on her ward at nine-fifteen p.m. blocking her way. And looking gorgeous and wildly sexy with his come-away-with-me eyes.

'I might ask you the same question.' Those eyes narrowed as he rocked back on his heels. 'They told me you were off duty—' he checked his watch '—fifteen minutes ago.'

A thread of annoyance wound through the surprise. So now she had to account for her whereabouts? What had happened to the no-strings clause? 'We're busy tonight.' He didn't need to know she'd volunteered an extra hour every night for the past few days because *she didn't want to see him. Didn't want to think about him.*

Especially not his full lips with their signature almost-smile. But from a few feet away she remembered how those lips had felt against hers. His taste spun through her head, that smoky turned-on tone of his voice raced through her veins.

He wore the black leather jacket he'd worn to Luna Park and she knew just how it felt against her fingers. Warm from his skin, soft as whipped cream. She wondered what would happen if she took those few steps closer and relived those few moments.

If she burrowed into that tempting strip of exposed T-shirt beneath the jacket and walked her hands beneath its hem—

She jerked her gaze away, curled her fingers around the tray of medication she held.

'One of my little patients isn't settling well tonight and I'm sitting with her. I was just getting her something to help her sleep.' She adjusted the medication on the tray.

'What time do you expect to get off?' he asked, with the confidence of a man who expected things to fall into place just because it suited him. Or was it because he had a free night and they hadn't had sex in four days and—she did a quick calculation—eleven hours.

'An hour,' she lied. 'Or two.'

A furrow formed between his brows. 'That's not true. The staff at the desk informed me you're only helping out, and I've made plans for the evening.'

'Plans?' It sounded tempting, especially spoken in that low, rumbling voice, and a perverse part of her wanted to toss away the medication along with her soft-soled shoes and skip out with him. 'Why didn't you ring first?'

'I wanted to surprise you.'

'Well, you did.' She started walking, moving to one side to pass him, but he stepped in front of her, his smooth coat-sleeve brushing her bare arm, a whiff of fresh masculine soap greeting her nostrils. She jerked her chin up to glare at him, but softened when her gaze connected with his. How could she turn him down? Even if seeing him would make it harder later, to let him go? 'Sorry, I've got to get this to Judy.'

'I'll wait.' He jammed his hands in his pockets and stepped aside.

She felt his eyes on her as she continued down the corridor until she turned the corner. When he could no longer see her, she stopped, leaned a hip against an unoccupied gurney.

Her pulse raced, she had to steady her breathing. The spine-tingling, heart-grabbing thrill of seeing him there, as if she'd summoned him up by thought alone, raced through her body. What was this all about? She'd heard nothing from him since the day his parents had arrived. Now he'd turned up at her place of work with Plans.

'Melanie.' A senior staff member approached, tapping her watch—obviously in cahoots with Luke. 'You're off duty as of fifteen minutes ago.' She took the tray from Melanie's hands and smiled at her over her spectacles. 'Visiting hours are over, young lady, and there's an attractive man waiting impatiently at the nurses' station. Go home.' She winked. 'Better still, go home with Mr Tall Dark and Handsome.'

CHAPTER TWELVE

'I'M NOT dressed for an evening out.' Melanie huddled in her old purple sheepskin as Luke drove them through the city. She'd worn denim and a baggy old windcheater intending to go straight home tonight.

He glanced at her, his eyes glittering with promise in the dashboard lights. 'You don't need to be for what I have in mind.'

She had an all-too-clear idea of what that was. But a voice of caution whispered through her veins and over the impatient drum of her heart. Now that his parents had settled in, she was being invited back into his life. For how long?

Each time she looked into Luke's deep dark eyes, would it be her last? She directed her gaze ahead and watched Sydney's shimmering lights bleed into the road's surface in strands of liquid colour as a rain-shower swept over the city.

Could she enjoy what they had, content to live each moment with him to the fullest, and be happy while it lasted? *Live the adventure,* her inner voice whispered.

Only one way to find out.

Luke came to an abrupt halt in the dining room. They both stared at the china and crystal, the unlit candle, the clutch of violets he'd picked from the garden on a whim.

At the time the rose plates had seemed like a good idea. His neck burned and he shifted his shoulders, uncomfortable with the whole romantic set-up. He wished like hell he'd just booked a table in town like any other male he knew would.

'Oh, Luke. Are we having an intimate supper?'

He felt Melanie come up beside him, but he couldn't look at her. Stupid, he knew, but the scene was so damn…feminine. He cleared his throat. 'I know. It's…'

'Romantic. And very sweet.' He felt her hand on his forearm. 'You even borrowed your mum's china for me.'

'Ah…no. That's mine.' By God, why had he gone and said that?

She blinked, obviously surprised. 'O…kay.'

'The sales girl told me women go for that sort of stuff.'

'Most women do.' She blinked again. 'I do,' she corrected quickly. Too quickly. Her hand tightened on his arm. 'You bought crockery to please me.'

He shrugged, confused, embarrassed, and crossed his arms. 'Hell, Melanie, I don't know what pleases you. I don't know where I am with you.'

And that had always been the attraction—and the dilemma. Melanie was different from any other woman he'd known. She never failed to surprise him.

She lifted her face and met his eyes. Her gaze melted into his, her lush lips puckered as she leaned closer. 'You're doing pretty well so far.'

He nodded, but stepped back, giving himself breathing space, because that was what the room seemed to be lacking at the moment—oxygen. 'That's the point of this exercise.'

'Exercise?' She straightened, a perplexed little frown forming on her brow. 'What do you mean?'

'I want to know you. I want you to know me.'

'I thought we knew each other pretty well already.'

'That's just it—we know each other's erogenous zones, but what else do we know? For instance, what's my favourite movie? What's yours? How do I feel about extra-terrestrial colonisation? Do you like walking on the beach in the rain?'

She looked at him as if to say, *Why do we need to know this when all we really need to know is how many different ways can we pleasure each other?*

Or perhaps she was simply reading his own mind, he decided as his eyes drifted to the loose top she wore and his fingers tingled… He cleared his throat. 'Mel, tonight's an experiment. No sex…'

'No sex, huh?' Her expressive eyes dimmed a little.

He reached out, traced the line of her jaw. 'Honey, it's only for tonight. Not because I don't want it, but because I want to explore us in a different way. Can we do that?'

She nodded slowly, a dubious half-grin on her lips. 'We can try. The question is why?'

He didn't want to answer that because he wasn't sure yet if he even had an answer. 'Just play along with me, okay?'

An eyebrow arched. 'Play? Okay,' she said when he didn't answer. The spark of challenge in her eyes seared him to the spot. 'My favourite movie is *Pretty Woman* and I love walking on the beach in the rain. Yours is *2001: A Space Odyssey*, and if you'd been fifty years younger you'd probably be the first geologist on the first manned mission to the red planet.' She rubbed her hands. 'So, now we've got that sorted, what's for supper, Romeo?'

Luke's jaw dropped open as he watched her saunter into the kitchen. Lucky guess? 'Okay, what's the name of the pet dog I had when I was twelve?'

'Meteor. Face it, Luke, you're well and truly trounced. Ooh, yum,' she murmured as she opened the refrigerator and peered inside.

He propped his shoulder on the door frame and watched as she leaned over and in, the curve of her bottom bobbing in a way that made his whole body tighten. He instantly regretted his plans for a romantic, *no-sex* evening. He continued watching as she backed out and straightened with a slice of the sticky pineapple dessert between her fingers.

She held it up. 'Have you become a gourmet cook in your absence?'

He pushed away from the door frame. 'I wish I could take the credit, but I'm still a toasted-sandwich guy…' Her tongue darted out to sample the toffee coating, and his own mouth watered.

A playful grin tipped up one corner of her mouth as she lifted the pineapple. 'I knew that—Cheddar cheese and Vegemite. This is good, Luke,' she said between tiny licks and bites that had him imagining her putting those caramel-glossed lips and teeth to another kind of good...

'Want a bit?' She licked her lips again. 'How about some of that cream on it?' And without waiting for a reply, she leaned in again and scooped up a dollop.

Ah, hell. The thought of taking her fingers in his mouth, tasting her on the fruit, slid through his mind, warm and syrupy and delicious. Everything inside him heated, pleaded, and he licked lips that had suddenly turned dry.

She must have seen the image too because she suddenly went very still beside the open refrigerator door, the cream-topped pineapple poised in front of her.

He almost groaned. The erotic foreplay of finger food—Mel and he could've written a book about it. The memories of their love feasts spiced the air between them, sending hot darts of need to his nerve endings.

Without taking her eyes off his, she approached him until he could see the charcoal ring around her irises. His gaze dipped to a freckle below her full bottom lip. He could smell her, a sensual fragrance you didn't find in a bottle.

As she lifted the morsel he opened his mouth, letting her fingers graze his lips. He leaned in as the sweet flavours of fruit and cream slid over his tongue.

He wanted the more tempting flavour of Melanie but she pulled back, smiling temptation's smile and licking the stickiness from her fingers. 'No sex—your rule, remember?'

'Food isn't sex,' he growled, but he knew better, and, from Mel's raised eyebrows and cheeky expression, so did she.

He stalked to the fridge and pulled out the prepared meal. 'Okay, let's eat—the traditional way.'

Traditional? Luke chewed on a spring roll but he barely

tasted it. How could eating while watching Melanie dip and swirl her own spring roll in sauce then slowly raise it to her lips and almost caress it before she bit off a mouthful be termed traditional? Did she have to make everything an exercise in eroticism?

But he managed to get through the meal. He even remembered to light the candle and pour the wine, and managed to make some sort of conversation, although he couldn't recall what he said if his life depended on it.

But he could remember what Melanie ate, *how* she ate, how she made love to the stem of her wine glass with those long slender fingers. How she watched his mouth as he chewed.

She was baiting him.

As soon as she'd patted her mouth, folded her cloth napkin and placed it to one side, he rose and stalked to the living room. Anything to get the blood that had pooled in his groin moving again.

He watched the rain blow over the harbour. Listened to the beat of his pulse over the sound as it drummed against his picture windows. He'd miscalculated. Badly.

The prickle on the back of his neck should have been a warning. He turned, bumping into lush, feminine curves.

'Great meal,' she said, looking up at him with sultry eyes. 'Thanks.'

'You're welcome.' Her scent and her body heat were twining their way through his senses. His pulse stepped up a notch but his blood remained below his belt. She might be wearing a shapeless windcheater, but he knew what she looked like underneath all that jersey. How she'd feel if he slipped his hands underneath...

His plan went into meltdown. His brain went into meltdown because when he ordered his legs to move his body simply bent from the waist and his mouth opened and fused to hers.

Her slick caramel-coated tongue darted out to meet his. His hands rose to set her away, but they merely curled around her arms and held on. *Not in the plan!*

Somehow, he managed to lift his head. A shred of sanity returned, reminding him that this whole no-sex deal had been his idea. His rule. And he was the one breaking it. He dragged in oxygen, short, sharp bursts that rasped over his dry throat.

Melanie stared up at him with dazed, passion-filled eyes, her own heavy breathing drawing attention to her kiss-moist lips, the rapid rise and fall of her breasts. 'What do we do now, Mr Plan Ahead?'

He locked his jaw, grabbed her hand and started walking. 'Get your coat.' He tugged her to the front door, snatching up a couple of umbrellas in the foyer. 'We're driving to the nearest beach and then we're going to take that long wet midnight walk in the rain that you love so much.'

'You want *me* to come to your welcome home party?' Melanie stared at him, the last bite of her chocolate éclair poised halfway to her pursed lips.

Luke had had a feeling she'd be less than enthusiastic, which was why he'd brought the Bribe—a selection of Mel's favourite French pastries from the local patisserie. 'It goes without saying. Of course I want you there.'

'At your parents' house.' Still watching him with a you've-got-to-be-kidding look on her face, she popped the rest of the treat into her mouth.

'That's the plan.' He'd waited until two p.m., knowing she'd put in a hard day's night at work, and had hoped for a more positive response. He wanted her to meet his parents so he could prove they weren't the ogres she obviously thought them to be. More, he wanted his parents to meet Melanie.

'And of course I want you to come. My parents are expecting you. All the family friends will be there.'

Pushing away from the table without a word, she crossed to the tiered clothes airer and picked up a towel, smoothing it with quick strokes and folding it into three.

Not a promising start.

'You accepted for me already, then?' She turned to him, the

towel clasped against her breast. *To the hired help's daughter rubbing shoulders with his friends.*

He could almost hear her unspoken words. He met her eyes, an indignant steel-grey, and clenched his jaw against his own rising exasperation. 'I'm asking you to come. My parents are who they are. They're a part of who I am, Melanie.'

But he wanted her acceptance—he hadn't realised until this moment how badly. 'You're a part of my life,' he said, softening his voice. He took the windcheater she'd picked up and dropped it on the sofa. Placed his hands on her stiff shoulders, looked into her eyes, willing her to believe him. 'A good part. And *I* want you there. Is that clear enough?'

She blinked at him, the steel in her eyes melting, but wariness creeping in to take its place. 'I don't know how to—' she gave a royal wave '—play the part.'

He squeezed her shoulders, tipped up her chin. 'You don't have to play at anything. Just be yourself. I can take you shopping, buy you a dress...' *Shopping?* Was he mad? For female clothing, no less. Underwear, no problem, he could deal with that, but a dress? Had he ever seen Melanie in a dress?

'What's wrong with my clothes?' Her voice rose a notch as she stepped back.

'I thought you might like something new.'

'I'm perfectly fine with what I've got. Thank you.'

'Good. Great.' He shrugged, shoving his useless hands in his pockets. This was trickier ground to negotiate than that excavation pit that had gone wrong last year.

She let out a resigned sigh. 'Um...so, what *is* the dress code for something like this? Formal? Casual?'

He hadn't given it a thought. Didn't women know instinctively what to wear? 'Whatever you feel comfortable in. Perhaps you could leave the fur boots and sheepskin jacket at home...'

'Give me *some* credit, Luke.' Her mouth curved ever so slightly. 'And I'm sure I can borrow a tiara from someone. I lost mine at the last ball I attended.'

He leaned forward so her mouth was a tempting nip away.

So he could smell her skin, the chocolate on her breath. 'I don't think that'll be necessary.'

Slowly, gently, he put his lips against hers and she yielded with a 'mmm' that hummed against his mouth and curled with a quiet warmth around his heart. A few nights ago he'd learned the uncomfortable way that sex wasn't the only thing keeping them together.

The following night they'd more than made up for it.

His hands rose to frame her jaw, his fingers tracing the dew-soft skin while he held her face still for his kiss. Licking the stickiness from her lips until she opened for him and let him into her moist, sweet mouth. While he watched her eyes change from the glint of polished pewter to the soft grey of summer mist.

He eased back a fraction, away from that lazy-lipped temptation to murmur, 'I'd really like to see you in a dress.' Something floaty, off-the-shoulder, so he could glide his fingers over her smooth skin. 'And some sexy stiletto shoes like you wore to the pub.' So he could admire the shape of her calves. 'But the decision's yours. You'll look good in whatever.'

'I'll see what I can do,' she said in a husky, sleepy voice that whispered over his chin and reminded him of lazy mornings in bed when she'd whispered those words. Her soft eyes held a glint of wickedness. 'What colour underwear should I wear, do you think?'

He smiled, remembering her seductive selection. 'Surprise me.'

The glint sharpened. 'I think I can manage that.'

His smile broadened. Melanie could always be counted on to surprise him.

CHAPTER THIRTEEN

ALL too soon the car Luke had hired to collect Melanie pulled to a smooth stop in the Delaneys' curved driveway. She rubbed sweaty palms together and watched the middle-aged couple caught in the car's headlights, squinting for a closer look at what the woman was wearing beneath her coat.

Melanie had decided on gypsy—full amethyst crushed-velvet skirt with matching clingy three-quarter sleeved sweater and a lacy turquoise and lavender top that tied between her breasts. She'd even used tongs to give her hair a flyaway look.

'Here we are, Ms Sawyer,' the driver said, stepping out and coming around to open her door.

'Thanks.' Melanie smiled at the guy as she climbed out, half tempted to ask him to take her home again.

She'd kept him waiting while she'd changed outfits three times and now the party seemed to be in full swing. Not swing, exactly—formal classical music drifted across the formal lawn with its formal fountain… Heat crept up her neck. Oh, yeah, *that* fountain.

Her only escape departed with a quiet engine hum, leaving her with no alternative but to face the inevitable. Her black stilettos clicked over the paving as she made her way towards the massive front door with its stained-glass roses. She'd had sex with Luke up against that door. Was there any place here that didn't remind her of those days?

But that had been when Luke was living alone. The music had been loud and hot, the sex sizzling. Apprehension twisted her insides into tight little knots. What did she have in common with these other people? Why had she agreed to come?

Before she could think about changing her mind and ringing for a taxi, the front door opened and Luke appeared, his large body lit by the foyer's sparkling chandelier.

At the bottom of the steps she lifted a hand and watched, her heart squeezing tight, a lump rising in her throat while he took the steps two at a time to meet her. He was wearing dark trousers, and his cream shirt accentuated his tanned skin, his smile bright against the darkness as he approached.

He was why she'd come. He was the only reason.

She pressed a fist against the pain in her chest as he drew near enough for her to see the clear and honest pleasure in his eyes at seeing her.

'Hi. Thank God you're here to keep me company.' He grabbed her fingers as he leaned down for a quick meeting of lips, smelling faintly of beer and something forest-fresh and fancy. 'Your hand's freezing—come on inside.' Keeping her hand in his, he tucked it beneath his arm and led her up the steps. Even with her hand in Luke's solid grip, her legs trembled, her insides quivered.

Elizabeth Delaney stood in the foyer, a pretty blonde woman in an elegant sky-blue silk top and slim-fitting black trousers, perfectly coiffed and made-up.

She smiled at Melanie, as openly and honestly as Luke as he squeezed her hand. 'Mum, I'd like you to meet Melanie Sawyer. Mel, this is Mum.'

'Good evening, Mrs Delaney.'

'Good evening, Melanie, and call me Elizabeth. I'm so pleased you were able to come.'

'Not as pleased as me,' Luke said, giving Melanie's hand another squeeze.

'It's lovely to meet you. We rarely meet any of Luke's girl-friends.'

Girlfriends. Plural. Melanie thought of the man by her side.

Yes, Luke would have had plenty of girlfriends. And she reminded herself that was all she was.

They'd shared something special over the past few weeks—at least it had been to her, even if she'd tried to pretend it was casual—but they'd shared other nights in the past. Wonderful, passionate nights when she'd naïvely thought in a secret corner of her heart their relationship could have been more.

'Have you known Luke long?' His mother's words brought her back to the present.

'We met five years ago, the last time he was in Sydney. I was serving at your husband's cocktail party.'

Luke slung an arm around Melanie. 'We're getting reacquainted.'

'You kept in touch these past few years, then?' Elizabeth frowned at her son. 'Shame on you, Luke, you never mentioned Melanie in your correspondence.'

Melanie's heart took a dive. Of course he'd never mentioned her, she'd been a fling. 'No,' she said, keeping her voice light. 'We didn't correspond. We bumped into each other again by chance.'

'Fate,' Luke said, his dark gaze drifting over her, but then with an 'excuse me a moment,' he moved away when a distinguished-looking man waved at him.

Left alone with his mother, Melanie pasted on a smile, forced herself to make conversation. 'Luke's been busy, hasn't he? You must be very proud.'

'Oh, yes, we are.' Elizabeth's gaze hovered on her son before returning to Melanie. 'I'm afraid these occasions aren't much to his liking, but his father insisted on welcoming him back.'

'You'll be happy to have him home.'

'Yes, but since he's found his own place we haven't seen as much of him as we'd have liked.' She studied Melanie a moment before Luke joined them again. 'I'm sure you'll be able to keep him occupied this evening,' Elizabeth said.

'I'm sure she will.'

At his husky tone, Melanie glanced up at Luke. The spark in

his eyes gave Melanie all kinds of possible scenarios for doing just that.

'Get your friend a drink, Luke, and mingle,' she told him.

Luke snagged two champagnes from a passing waiter, handed her one. 'To you.' He clinked his glass to hers. 'You look sensational.'

'Thanks.' She took a tiny sip to moisten her dry mouth.

Then he leaned nearer and whispered in her ear, 'Makes me wonder what lingerie you're wearing underneath.'

Anticipation fizzed through her blood but she forced all thoughts of his hands on her lingerie away. 'Later. Where's your dad?'

She needn't have asked, because, like Luke, he stood out in the crowd, formally attired in black trousers, white shirt and striped tie. He stood by the fireplace, conversing with an elderly man whose back was towards her. Colin had obviously seen them come in and was watching them. Or more specifically, her.

'Over here,' said Luke. With a light hand on her back, he steered her through the guests.

Head up, smile. Make an effort. This is Luke's dad.

When they reached his side, Colin inclined his head and extended his hand as Luke introduced her. 'Call me Colin. We've met before, haven't we? Good evening, Melanie.' His handshake was firm and mercifully brief.

'Good evening, Colin.'

He turned to the distinguished-looking man to his left and in a superior voice, said, 'You won't have met Sir Gerald Doyle—'

But the man was already enfolding Melanie in his arms. 'Melanie, it's good to see you.'

'Hello, Gerry, how are you?'

'Super. I'm even back playing tennis again.' His eyes twinkled at her as he stepped back, still gripping her hand.

'And how's Minette?' she asked, ultra-aware of Colin's surprised gaze on her.

'She's well, thank you. She's in Melbourne at present, visiting our son and his wife and our new granddaughter.'

'That'll make number three, won't it?'

'Indeed. Colin, this girl's an angel,' he went on, finally releasing her. 'When I had my heart attack last year she was on duty in Emergency. She helped save my life. Took a special interest in me and Minette when I was recovering.' He nodded at Luke. 'You're a lucky man.'

'I think so,' Luke said. Melanie felt his proprietary arm around her shoulders, almost as if Luke acknowledged Gerry's assumption that they were a couple. A more permanent couple.

'Nursing's a hard job,' Colin conceded with a grudging nod. 'You've obviously found your calling.'

Melanie's chin lifted, accepting the somewhat backhanded compliment with as much graciousness as she could muster. 'Yes. I have.'

'We'd better move on,' Luke said. 'Mum told us to mingle.'

'Lovely to see you again, Melanie. Minette'll be sorry she missed you.'

She smiled at the man she'd become firm friends with. 'Tell her I said hello and I'll call her soon.'

'I didn't think I'd see Gerry here,' she said, taking a sip of her drink as they moved away.

'Told you you'd fit right in.'

But Melanie didn't meet anyone else she knew. She recognised a few faces from the society pages as Luke introduced her to the seemingly endless parade of people.

Her fingers were stiff from clenching the glass, her cheeks ached from smiling, her feet throbbed from standing too long in too-high shoes. She found herself with a group of older women when Luke excused himself to speak with the wait staff about supper. Her brain reeled with names and faces and overheard gossip she wasn't privy to, including a Botox disaster, two affairs and a marriage break-up.

Every time she looked away hoping to catch a glimpse of Luke on his way back to rescue her, she found Colin's eyes assessing her and no doubt finding her lacking, if his frown was any indication.

At the moment, however, he was talking to a press photographer Melanie had seen arrive a few moments ago and a stunning young blonde in a strapless red dress. She saw him beckon someone—Luke, she realised with a sinking feeling in the pit of her stomach—and introduce them. Saw Blondie smile, saw Luke bend down and speak. So they were head to head.

Her fingers tightened on her glass and her insides clenched as Blondie pressed against Luke's side and posed for the camera. Luke's hand was on her bare shoulder. The flash caught them as Blondie turned her head to smile up at Luke's face. He said something to her and smiled back.

Luke's gaze suddenly switched to Melanie, as if he knew she was watching, but she was already excusing herself to the women she'd been talking to and turning away. She refused to stand here and watch her partner for the evening—*hers*—photographed with someone else. Particularly someone as gorgeous as that woman.

Time out. Dumping her glass on the nearest surface, she escaped into the hall. With a quick glance behind her, she headed for the library. 'Hello?' she half whispered as she pushed on the heavy door. Only the familiar and faint musty smell of old leather and books greeted her. Thank God.

Releasing a pent-up sigh, she closed the door behind her, let her head fall back against the polished wood for a few seconds while her eyes adjusted to the pale moonlight streaming like silver through the window.

Pull yourself together. That was Colin's doing, not Luke's.

Problem was, it was as blindingly clear as that moonlight that Melanie Sawyer was jealous. She'd never been jealous in her life, but she recognised the symptoms. She was jealous because...

Oh, no. No, no, no. She *couldn't* be in love with Luke Delaney.

Not again.

A man she'd do anything for—even attend this stupid party she didn't fit into.

A man whose world she didn't belong in.

No, she'd done 'in love', she was *not* doing it again. It was going to be casual all the way.

'Mel?'

She almost stumbled when the door opened, propelling her forward. 'Here.'

Her heart hammered at the sound of that same man's deep voice. With his body silhouetted against the light from the hall, all she could see was his familiar shape as he entered the room and closed the door.

Now she could see his shirt gleaming in the moon's glow, his eyes glinting with concern. 'I apologise for Dad's insensitivity. He was introducing me to a friend's granddaughter. I didn't know about the photo shoot.'

Ignore that burning sensation in your chest, the temptation to blame. Stick to the facts. 'He obviously thinks you two are well suited. She's very attractive.'

'I didn't notice,' he said, reaching for her, fingers curling around her nape and urging her closer, making her forget about everything but him. 'You see, I prefer long-legged brunettes.'

Melanie leaned forward, her own fingers busy undoing the top two buttons of his shirt so she could slip her fingers inside and feel the hot flesh beneath. 'Ah, so you did notice she was blonde, then.'

'I *noticed* you leave.' His hands stroked over her shoulders and down her spine as he walked her backwards until her bottom bumped into the antique desk.

'But I didn't leave…the party…'

Her breathing hitched mid-sentence when he cupped her backside in his palms and lifted her onto the desk. 'No.' His voice whispered over her face. 'You didn't.'

'Want to know why?' She kicked off her shoes and watched the glint in his eyes turn hot while she tugged at his chest hair. 'You haven't checked out my underwear yet.'

'But I've been thinking about it all night.' She felt the texture of velvet, then cool air kissed her thighs as he pushed her skirt up over her knees. Spread them wide.

'Black stockings…' The rough edges of his fingers snagged nylon as he slid a hand between her thighs and up. 'Lace-topped,' he murmured when his fingers finally encountered flesh.

He inched higher, stopped, surprise and amusement crinkling his eyes. His fingers slid against her moist centre. 'You came bare-assed?'

She shivered with desire as heat met heat. 'I came prepared.'

'So did I.' He took a condom from his pocket with his free hand and grinned, his teeth white against his skin while his long, skilled fingers continued to slide back and forth over her flesh until she moaned. 'Want to take a chance, Mel?'

'Here?' In the library with a hundred guests only metres away? Her pulse leaped and adrenaline spiked at the idea.

'Now.' He slid her to the very edge of the desk, so her bottom perched precariously. Then cocked his brow. 'Do you want me to lock the door?'

She shook her head. 'Where's the thrill in that?'

He shrugged, still grinning. 'Didn't think so.' He unzipped his fly.

'Let me.' She shoved his hands away and reached between them, tightened her hand around him, feeling him jerk in response. Squeezing, she moved her hands slowly up, then down, watching his jaw clench, his eyes half close on a tight indrawn breath.

But their gazes locked as she took the condom packet from his fingers. Beyond the door she could hear Beethoven, the distant murmur of conversation, but the only sounds in the room were heavy breathing and the sharp rip of foil.

Still watching him, she rolled on the condom, then with hands tight on his rock-hard length she guided him closer, until his tip touched her swollen flesh.

'Ah, Melanie, I can never get enough of you,' he muttered,

gripping her thighs as he pushed inside her. Watching himself as he thrust his hips forward, her hands clutching his shoulders to keep herself from slipping off the desk. She watched too, the skin at the top of her thighs pale against his dark masculine power.

A power that could wring every emotion from her, body and soul. If she let it. Not tonight. Tonight it was only about illicit sex and its accompanying adrenaline rush and how very, very good they felt together.

The sensual storm erupted around her, a blistering explosion of skin and speed and heat, until nothing but the vortex of pure pleasure remained. She quivered on the edge, then let the pleasure take her. Luke followed her down as she collapsed backwards, letting her head drop back against the desk.

A lamp tipped and rolled onto its side with a tinkle of glass. 'Oops.'

Luke shifted, set the light upright. 'Just the globe,' he said. He adjusted his clothing in the dim light, swept up the pieces of broken glass with a tissue, tipped them in the bin. 'You okay?'

She smiled, feeling entirely too good to move. 'What do you think?'

He slid his lips over hers. Once, twice. 'I think we'd best get back to—'

High-pitched laughter was followed by the sounds of the door opening and two voices; one male, one female.

Quick as a flash Luke whipped her skirt down over her knees as she struggled up. In the anticipatory silence she could feel his hands on her thighs, could almost hear his heart beating over her own.

'I think we're safe,' the male voice murmured into the dimness.

'Ah, not quite, I'm afraid,' Luke said with a private moonlit grin only Melanie could see.

Meeting Luke's we're-in-this-together eyes, Melanie bit her lip, just tipsy enough to want to giggle, sober enough to keep that urge in check.

There was a pause, followed by a stifled gasp and a quick scuffle as the door closed.

'I don't know about you but that close call's made me hungry,' Luke said, scouring the carpet and retrieving Melanie's shoes.

She slid off the desk, smoothed her clothing, stepped into her shoes. 'I could do with a coffee. Do you think we've missed supper?'

'No. It's too early.' Luke zipped his fly, yanked his belt further up his waist then walked to the door, looked both ways. 'The coast's clear. What say we check out the kitchen instead?'

CHAPTER FOURTEEN

'Is that coffee I can smell fresh, Melanie?'

In the kitchen Melanie's high spirits plummeted. That arrogant boom could only belong to one man. Smile fixed in place, she turned. 'Colin.' And far too close. 'Yes, would you care for one? Luke's just gone to the bathroom—' to dispose of the condom '—he'll be back in a moment.'

He nodded. 'If it's not too much trouble.'

'Not at all.' She manoeuvred around busy wait staff to set another mug on the bench. 'How do you take it?'

'Black, no sugar.'

He leaned an upraised arm on the wall, an intimidating stance and near enough for Melanie to see the pulse beating in his throat, the glint in his dark eyes as they focused on hers. Sizing her up.

'Well, Melanie Sawyer, no more waiting tables, eh?'

The way he said it, as if hard honest work wasn't good enough, highlighted what she already knew of his prejudice. Or was it just her in particular he didn't like?

'No,' she replied. *Yet here I am fixing you coffee.*

'I'll have a few of those fish things—' he indicated one of the supper dishes with a flick of his wrist '—and a couple of sausage rolls. Plates are in that cupboard.' He leaned down so his breath stirred the hair at her brow and said, 'Between you and me, I don't trust the catering service's crockery.'

'Oh?' She almost shuddered at the thought of anything between her and Colin Delaney. Except…he'd almost been a grandfather to her baby… He was Luke's flesh and blood… She had to make it work between them.

She found a spatula on the bench and slid the requested savouries onto the requested clean plate. 'These guys have a high standard of hygiene…'

This man had also denied her the information to Luke's whereabouts. 'And I should know.' She set the plate beside his coffee with a firm thud and matched his gaze with a cool stare. 'I've worked with Class Catering.'

'Melanie.' Elizabeth stood in the doorway. She shot her husband a glance that said she'd been standing there quite long enough to get the drift—and tone—of the conversation, then smiled at Melanie. She held an elegant store-wrapped box. 'I hope my husband's looking after you. I was looking for Luke.'

'He's—'

'Right here, Mum.'

Melanie breathed an inaudible sigh of relief as Elizabeth turned to her son, diverting attention away from her. 'I picked you up a little something for your apartment today,' she said.

'Spencer Overton's here to discuss the plans for our new promotion, Luke,' Colin interrupted. 'He's leaving for the States tomorrow and I'd like you to be in on this. When you've got a spare moment, we'll be in the study.'

'I'll be right there.' Luke's eyes linked with Melanie's for a brief moment before he broke the connection and kissed his mother's cheek. 'Thanks, Mum.'

He slipped off the bow and ribbons, peeled away the shiny paper. 'Glasses.' He withdrew one and held it to the light where it sparkled.

Not just any glasses, Melanie noted. Famous brand, exquisitely cut crystal glasses on delicate stems, which put her own house-warming offering from the local chain store to shame. And a fancy silver corkscrew with a multi-faceted crystal knob on top.

She bit the inside of her lip. How could she hope to come up to scratch with this wealthy family?

But Luke's eyes were warm when he said, 'You can never have too many glasses.' He winked conspiratorially at her. 'Nor too many corkscrews.' His expression sobered. 'You okay?'

'Fine.' Melanie smiled. But she didn't feel fine. She felt sticky and tense and oh-so-aware of the draught of air beneath her skirt cooling her still-hot woman's flesh. Play with fire...

'I'd better go see what Dad wants.' Luke gave her a quick miss-me kiss before she could think of why this whole idea had been a mistake.

'Do you like to read, Melanie?' his mother asked as soon as Luke had gone.

'Yes, when I get time.'

Elizabeth led the way out of the kitchen and down the hall towards the library. 'We have a large collection of books here, if you'd like to borrow something some time.' She opened the door, switched on the light.

Melanie's gaze flew straight to the little table lamp on the desk, and she breathed a sigh of relief. All okay.

Elizabeth walked to the largest set of shelves, which covered one wall, and perused the titles, all first editions and leather-bound books—not a cheap paperback in sight.

'Poetry?'

As in...Blake? Browning? Melanie shook her head. 'No, poetry doesn't do it for me, I'm afraid.' Nor did most of the classic authors. Did that automatically ostracise her?

'Any particular authors? Genres?'

Melanie shook her head. 'Anything with good characterisation, and I like an unexpected plot twist.'

Elizabeth nodded, still studying the shelves. 'These are all Colin's books, or they've been handed down through the family. I like a good romance myself.' She crossed to an antique oak cabinet, opened a door and withdrew a handful of well-read paperbacks.

Melanie studied the covers—windswept landscapes, sultry women in sexy lingerie on silken sheets. Hot, hard men with their hands on voluptuous female flesh. She picked up a familiar book. 'This is one of my favourite authors.'

'So you like a happy ending too.'

'Yes.' Melanie thought of her and Luke and her stomach tangled into a hard knot. A happy ending wasn't in her future. She didn't fit in here with first editions and lead-crystal glasses. Not that it mattered-no-strings Luke was strictly temporary. At least that had always been crystal clear. 'But this is fantasy,' Melanie said, setting the book down. 'Real life's not like that.'

'No, it's not,' Elizabeth said slowly. She paced a few steps away, then turned. 'I worry about Luke. It's a mother's prerogative, I guess,' she said with a hint of a smile. 'He's a soft centre, easily hurt.'

A rose-cream-smothered-in-dark-chocolate man. Melanie knew.

'Over the years he's become an expert at hiding his emotions,' Elizabeth continued. 'But with you this evening…it's obvious how he feels about you. He couldn't wait till tonight to show you off, and he may not have mentioned it to me, but I know he was afraid you might not come.' Her vivid blue eyes assessed Melanie. 'I'd hate to see him hurt.'

Ah, the lioness protecting her own. 'So would I.' Melanie heard the snip in her voice. And what about your husband? she wanted to ask. How would Luke feel knowing his father had refused to put her in touch, that Luke had never had the chance to be a part of her pregnancy? 'Luke and I are…close friends, we both understand, and value, our relationship.'

Elizabeth nodded as if satisfied with that answer—for now—and switched topics. 'And you, Melanie? I understand how hard it must have been to lose your parents. Your mother was a loyal employee and a hard worker. You've worked hard too, to get where you are.'

'Yes.' *And do you really understand all that?*

Elizabeth must have read Melanie's expression because she lifted a shoulder and her blue eyes clouded, her lips turned down at the corners. 'My father was a factory worker, my mother took in ironing.' Her voice was firm, matter-of-fact. 'He worked hard and struggled every day of his life till a heart attack took him, leaving my mother with two small children.'

Melanie's breath caught and she instantly regretted the bite in her tone. 'I'm sorry. I didn't know.'

Because Luke had never told her.

'How did you meet your husband?'

'I worked as a cashier in his first restaurant. When he had some success he promoted me to his office as a personal assistant.' Her voice softened with time-honoured memories. 'It was a long time ago. I just wanted you to understand before… Before you two make any important decisions.' Something sad drifted across her smile, then her eyes brightened and she said, 'What say we drag Luke away from business and get some supper?'

'Let me come over after I've finished up here.' Luke opened the chauffeured car door for Melanie, catching a whiff of her perfume, the bump of a shoulder as she climbed in.

'Not tonight. I'm on duty at seven tomorrow morning. I need to sleep.'

'I'll let you sleep—' he whispered in her ear, unable to resist a nibble '—after.'

She lifted her mouth for another goodnight kiss. 'No.' But she smiled as she said it.

'Okay, in that case I'll stay here overnight, get an early start on clearing out the rest of my gear. There are boxes that go back years. If you change your mind at three a.m.…'

She grinned. 'See you Saturday afternoon.'

'Ah, the baby shower.'

'You have to keep Ben company.'

'I hardly know the guy.'

'Good reason to keep him company, then.'

She didn't change her mind, which Luke decided was probably a good thing, since he ended up spending Friday helping his mum take down curtains, take out rugs. Spring cleaning in the middle of winter. God knew they could have employed their cleaning service for some extra hours but Mum wanted to do it herself, and Luke was all for letting her, except he was the one doing most of the work, wasn't he?

He didn't mind at all. Mum had never forgotten her roots and every so often she reverted to the woman she must have been before she married. Doing everything herself. Getting her hands dirty. He wondered if it had something to do with the talk she and Mel had been having in the library. She didn't seem inclined to discuss it.

Which was fine, he thought, dumping the last few cartons from his old room into the boot of his car to sort through later. They had more in common than perhaps they realised at present and that had to be progress.

Normally Luke didn't mind being the only male in a roomful of women. But not when one of those women looked dangerously ready to give birth at any moment… He shuddered at the thought.

'Mel's not here yet?' He accepted a bottle of beer some woman—Sophie? Sylvie?—pressed into his hand.

'No,' Sophie/Sylvie said with a smile. 'Would you like to wait in here for her?'

Good God, no.

'She was supposed to come off duty at seven,' Carissa said. 'But there was a staffing problem, she didn't get off till a couple of hours ago. She'll be here soon, Luke.'

'She worked last night *and* this morning? She'll be knackered,' he replied, incredulous that the hospital allowed such overtime. Not letting his eyes stray to that very distended belly beneath the patterned shirt. Conscious that the women knew he was uncomfortable. Wishing Ben were there to lead him to somewhere safe.

Wise man Ben was keeping his distance.

But no. As if his wish had been granted, Ben appeared in

the kitchen doorway. His gaze slid over his wife's belly, then lingered. 'You feeling okay? No more twinges?'

'No, I'm fine. Stop hovering. Luke's here.'

Ben's gaze swung towards him. 'Hey, Luke.' He beckoned with his beer bottle. 'This way, mate.'

Luke couldn't get out of there fast enough. He followed Ben outside and into the welcome afternoon sunshine.

'This is some backyard,' he said, taking in the lush lawn and young fruit trees, bare now, but come summer they'd be green and in a few years would provide shade. A row of euca-lypts, their leaves glossy in the sun, screened the back of the property.

'Great for kids,' Ben said.

As in plural? 'You intend to have more than one?' Luke stared at him, wondering how this man, who'd been practi-cally a music legend back in XL Rock's days, could be a fam-ily man.

'Oh, yeah.' Ben grinned. 'We want at least three.'

'Jeez.' Luke hid a shudder, thinking of Carissa's belly again.

The thought of Melanie, pregnant with his child, slid through his mind before he could block it, and another more powerful sensation powered through him, leaving him dazed.

His child inside Mel. With dark hair and Mel's misty grey eyes. Mischievous and full of life. Oh, yeah, he'd imagined get-ting her that way, but this time it was something much deeper.

He shook his head, took a long swig from his bottle and let the cold yeasty taste soothe his suddenly dry throat. Comforted himself with the thought that Mel wasn't the maternal type. *Single and loving it*. Hadn't she said it herself? Hadn't she dem-onstrated that over and over?

'How do you stand it?' He gestured towards the house where the sounds of feminine laughter rippled on the air. 'Seeing your wife like that and knowing what's going to happen.'

'Yeah.' Ben's expression sobered. 'I wasn't there when she lost the baby, so this'll be a first for me. But watching her grow, following the baby's progress…it's really been an experience not to be missed.'

Luke nodded. All unfamiliar territory for him.

'Carissa's loved it,' Ben went on. 'Well, most of the time. It's harder now, with a couple weeks left. But women seem to take it in their stride. They're built for it, and I've never seen my wife look more beautiful. I can't stop touching her, you know?'

No. Luke didn't know. Didn't want to know. 'I don't mind telling you it scares the bejeezus out of me.'

'When you find the woman you want to spend the rest of your life with you'll change your mind. Not the fear,' he went on. 'That's natural, you don't want to see the woman you love in pain while you watch damn helpless—but you'll want to share a child, you want that connection.'

'I'll take your word for it.' Luke tossed him a look, but he doubted Ben heard—his eyes had already glazed over.

Luke blew out a breath and hunched his shoulders as a gust of wind shivered through the trees. He didn't want to be having this conversation. 'So what's the work-in-progress?' He indicated what looked like a partially constructed shed.

Ben came back from whatever planet he'd been on and said, 'A kid's cubby.'

'Bit early, isn't it?'

'So I've been told.' He took a gulp of his beer. 'I always wanted one as a kid. Couldn't afford it and Dad wouldn't have motivated himself enough to build one. I'll probably get as much pleasure out of it as the child.'

Luke eyed Ben with interest. Judging from the bitter tone, the hard jaw and harder eyes, Ben hadn't gotten along with his dad. He'd grown up without money, so he'd made his fortune on his own.

'Well, if Carissa kicks you out you can always use it as a doghouse.'

Ben laughed as if that notion was absurd before resuming

his granite-eyed expression. 'If there's one thing I want to do in my life, it's to be a good father.'

In the long silence that followed Luke sensed the man's hard-edged determination. What constituted a good father? he asked himself. Was he judging his own unfairly? Or had Dad's relentless push been based on purely self-motivated needs?

'You and Mel got any plans?' Ben finally asked with a side-ways glance.

Plans? Mel lived for the day, the moment. She didn't do plans. He shrugged, oddly uneasy with the way the question made him feel—hurt, empty. Alone. 'You know Mel.'

'Yeah. Loads of fun, but a dedicated workaholic.'

Luke made an effort at lightness. 'You know the rule—work hard, play hard.'

'With all the overtime she puts in, it doesn't leave much time for play.'

One corner of Luke's mouth tipped up at Ben's lifted brow. 'Oh, we make time.'

And when she did come out to play…

Luke's mind spun back to their last playtime, in the parents' library. Mel's particular favourite—the adrenaline rush that came from knowing they might be caught out at any moment.

His body grew hard just thinking about it again. Oh, yeah, she knew how to play.

But was play enough?

Luke didn't have time to ponder that because Mel pushed out of the back door with a plate of cupcakes rolled in jelly and coconut.

He watched her descend the steps with something close to pain around his heart at that first unexpected jolt of seeing her again. Wearing red thigh-high boots, an itty-bitty denim skirt and red jumper with yellow snowflakes cascading across her breasts, she looked like sunshine on a winter's day and wore a smile to match.

'Hi,' he said. 'You made it.'

'Of course. I wouldn't miss my sister's baby shower… Is something wrong?'

Not if you didn't count the shadows beneath her eyes. 'Now you're here?' He made a deliberate effort to smile. 'Not a thing.'

'Oh, good, 'cos I remembered how you love jelly cakes. I just made them and if I don't bring you guys some now those vultures in there will devour them.'

'You *just made them?* I thought you'd be taking a nap.'

'No time. Besides, if I stop then I drop. Better to push on.' She held out the plate. The aroma of fresh cake mingled with Mel's fragrance.

'We were just talking about play,' he said, taking the plate and leaning into her neck for a better sample. Meeting her eyes with unspoken memories of the other night. 'Ben and I agree you don't have enough.' Didn't matter that Luke himself often put in eighteen-hour days; he wasn't rushed off his feet with people's lives in his hands.

'Oh?' Her eyes glinted with silver promises, her voice dropped to a husky tone that played havoc with Luke's libido. 'We can play later.' She pressed a warm, hard kiss on his lips, whirled towards the door. 'Gotta go.'

'Was she always like that when you knew her before?' Ben said as they watched the fly-screen door slap behind her.

'Yep. A lightning ball of energy. Till she crashes, then it's goodnight sleep tight.' He hadn't been able to put his finger on it, but there *was* something different about Mel this time round.

Luke wondered how far that energy would extend tonight. He'd been looking forward to some slow, get-serious love-making now that the initial burn had eased slightly.

Time to explore each other more fully, more intimately. Time to linger some more over the subtle changes, to reacquaint, to reconnect on a deeper level.

But tonight? The odds of exploring those changes were not in his favour.

* * *

'Are you sure I can't tempt you with some wine?' Ben paused, his bottle of Merlot poised over Luke's glass.

Luke covered his glass with a hand. 'No thanks, mate, I'm driving.'

The afternoon's party had finished an hour ago. Only Melanie remained and Luke wasn't leaving without her.

At the moment, Mel was nibbling on a party sausage roll, her attention wholly focused on Carissa. Which made Luke exceedingly nervous.

Ben moved to Melanie's side. 'Are you sure you won't try some, Mel?'

She glanced up at Ben. 'I'm right, thanks.'

'This is exquisite wine, purchased at great expense—don't tell me you don't want at least a taste.'

'Sorry, Ben, if I drink now I'll never make it home.'

And Luke very much wanted her home. Tucked up in bed beside him. 'I'll drive you,' he said.

'Good.' She slid him a potent look. 'Need to keep alert, then, don't I?'

He sat back with a sigh of anticipation. His place or hers, it didn't matter. He'd let her sleep as long as she needed because when she woke he wanted her as hungry for him as he was for her.

Right now though he was practically salivating over the last piece of black cherry cheesecake—there were different kinds of hunger.

'For heaven's sake, it's yours.' Melanie slid the entire cream-messed plate his way, then shot her sister a concerned look. 'Carrie?'

'Fine.' Carissa smiled, glanced at the digital display on the entertainment unit.

'You've been watching that clock for a while now,' Melanie said. 'I want to know why.'

'It's nothing. Just those Braxton Hicks contractions…'

'Contractions?' Luke felt his pulse speed up.

Ben was beside Carissa in an instant, his hands on her belly. 'Sweetheart, anything I can get you?'

'I'm all right.' She laughed and turned to Luke. 'It's okay, Luke, they're not painful and don't mean you're in labour.'

'Please don't say that word.'

'I never took Luke for a coward, did you, Mel?'

'No, but maybe I misjudged him.' She didn't spare him a glance. 'How far apart are those contractions?'

'Oh…a while…'

'Let me know if they become regular or more frequent. Do you want to ring the hospital and talk to them?'

'No. I'm not due for twelve days.'

'Doesn't mean a thing. Lots of women have said that right before they went into labour. At least come and sit on the sofa, you'll be more comfortable.'

'If I can ever get up again once I'm down there,' Carissa complained.

'You've got Ben to help you—men have to be useful for something, after all, he was the one that got you this way in the first place.'

'Yes.' She smiled at her husband, who smiled right back, but there was more devilment than dreams in those twinkling green eyes.

Carissa pushed up slowly and made her way to the sofa, sat with a sigh.

'Give me your feet.'

Luke watched Melanie's capable fingers slip Carissa's shoes off and begin a slow rhythmic massage. He couldn't repress an inward groan.

Not so long ago on that memorable getaway weekend she'd worked those fingers over his temples and neck. He was still waiting for her to work that slow sensual magic on other parts. Fast and furious was the only speed they knew at present.

'Did you see what Melanie brought us for the baby, Ben?' She pointed to the decorated basket on the piano. 'It's just the cutest little outfit you ever saw. And the purple stuffed koala with the joey on its back.'

'Yep, I can see Melanie's colour scheme here.' Ben tossed the little koala to Carissa.

'I could've got fur, but this one's washable. That's only for starters,' Melanie said, working her way up Carissa's calves. 'When we know the sex, I'll be buying up big time. There was this owl clock that blinks the seconds with big numbers so you can teach the time... Carrie?'

Luke's eyes switched to Carissa. She wasn't listening to Mel; her gaze was focused inward. As he watched she seemed to tense then let out an unsteady breath. He saw Mel put her palm on Carissa's belly.

'I need...Ben, help me up, I think I need...'

'Carrie?'

'I think my water just broke. There was a ping...' She let out a groan and clutched her sister's hand.

Luke felt the blood drain from his face.

Ben was beside his wife in three quick strides.

Mel switched to professional mode in the blink of an eye. 'Ben, ring the hospital, tell them we're on our way. Just how far apart are those contractions you've been timing, Carrie?'

'Two minutes, one minute. They weren't painful, I didn't think—'

'Ben, change of plans. Ring an ambulance.'

CHAPTER FIFTEEN

'Luke—' Melanie glanced at him and he could almost see her eyes roll heavenward. 'Go outside and wait for the ambulance.'

He was forced to admit it—he was glad to escape. Standing on the front porch, he strained his ears for any sign of a siren. How long did a damn ambulance take anyway?

'Ben-n-n…!'

His gut twisted at the sound of Carissa's anguished cry. Sweat snaked down his back. Imagining Mel going through this. For him… Suddenly it was as clear as sun through crystal: there'd never been another woman he'd wanted to make a baby with—it had only ever been about Melanie.

Melanie could have wept at the sound of the ambulance pulling up outside. In seconds two paramedics pushed through the door, loaded Carissa into the ambulance with a white-faced Ben beside her, and suddenly, after all the commotion, it was…quiet.

'Well…' She turned to Luke, trailed off, seeing him slumped against a pole, his complexion a bilious shade of green. Her heart melted, and, with her maternal instincts already painfully aroused, she reached out to him. 'Oh, Luke, honey…'

He pushed her hand away and for a millisecond his eyes flashed to hers. Pride and humiliation. She let him go, watching him weave his way inside with an ache that warmed her from the inside out.

A tense hour later, Ben rang Melanie with the news. Another hour passed before she and Luke were allowed into Carissa's room.

She saw her sister sitting up in bed, cradling her newborn infant, and wanted to weep. Tears of joy, with a few scattered through for a quiet sadness she'd come to terms with and accepted. 'Hi,' she whispered.

Carissa looked up, motherhood shining through her glazed eyes. 'Hi, you two!'

Ben gave a quick heads-up at the exchange, his attention focused on his wife and child.

'Come over here right now,' Carissa said, her voice scratchy and breathless.

Melanie wasted no time launching herself across the room to kiss her sister and get her first up-close look at the little miracle. 'You almost didn't make it here in time.'

'But we did, and everything's fine.'

'We have a son.' Ben's voice cracked on the last word. His hands weren't quite steady as he reached down to pick up the dark-haired, red-faced little mite from his mother's arms.

The sight of such a big man with the tiny fragile bundle against his chest brought a swift and powerful lurch to Melanie's pulse. The thought of Luke cradling a baby they'd made together crept through her veins and stole softly into her heart.

Ben tucked the blue flannelette beneath the baby's chin. 'Say hello to Robert Baxter Jamieson.'

'Luke, look.' She turned to see Luke hesitating near the door. For a brief moment she saw something cross his expression as he focused on mother and child. Happiness? Regret? Hope?

The same emotions echoed within her. She wanted to reach out and tell him all her own regrets and hopes for the future. A future with him. Her head spun with those thoughts; the joy of this birth would make it so much harder for him to hear of her own loss.

He hesitated. 'This is a family time…'

'You're a part of this,' she said gently, smiling at him through blurry eyes. 'Come and meet my nephew.'

Luke's whole demeanour softened as he got his first close-up look. 'Congratulations,' he said, his voice sounding oddly strained as he touched a finger to the tiny head. 'He's something, isn't he?'

'Doesn't he have the most beautiful eyes?'

'Look at those musician's fingers.'

Questions and compliments flowed and the joyful celebration lasted a full five minutes before a nurse came to check on mother and baby—a signal for Melanie and Luke to leave.

Luke drove Melanie back to her apartment. The moment she entered the door she bustled about her kitchen, cleaning up the mess from her cooking stint earlier. Her feet were numb, her brain number, she hadn't slept in more than twenty-four hours, but she was floating through some sort of euphoric haze. She was an auntie. Even more wonderful, Carissa was a mother at last.

'Come on, Melanie, leave the dishes. It's bedtime.'

She glanced around at the sound of that deep voice and found Luke leaning against the door jamb.

But something else stopped her in her tracks.

It wasn't the expected lust she saw in his eyes, which might have earned him a 'forget it, I'm bushed'. Although she doubted she'd have refused, even if it had been only about mutual needs and wants, because tonight she needed. Desperately.

No, it was something more, something deeper. A deeper respect perhaps? For women and women's work, for her career? Or was it as simple as Melanie Sawyer?

Her heart swelled and tumbled, her nose prickled. Holding that deep dark gaze with hers, she crossed to him. Touched his stubbled jaw, breathed in his masculine sweat-tainted shirt. 'Isn't it wonderful? A baby.'

He made a self-deprecating sound in his throat and shook his head. 'I don't know how you women do it. Why do you want to put yourselves through that?'

Why? 'For love, Luke.' *Don't you get that?*

'I don't think I could stand it, seeing you... If I ever made you pregnant...'

His words stabbed through her like a knife. Her heart stopped, then began again at double time. Why did he have to say that *now,* when she'd already framed the words she was going to use in her head? Later?

'Luke, it's okay,' she said quietly, loving him with every beat of her throbbing heart. Finally admitting what she'd always known. Why there'd never been anyone else for her but this man searching her eyes with such sweet tenderness.

But she'd not been honest with him. She should have persisted. Written again. Tried harder. She should have known Luke wasn't the kind of man who'd walk away from a child—*his* child—without a word, even if those words had been a rejection. And a rejection would have come with support, even if only a monetary one.

She'd misjudged him and denied him the opportunity.

'Hey. You're crying.' With the pads of his fingers he wiped the moisture from her cheeks that she hadn't realised was there.

'I am *not* crying.' But, dammit, she wanted to keep crying. Sheer determination kept the tears at bay.

'You're exhausted, you're over-emotional and you're going to bed.' He swept her up into his arms and placed his lips on hers, a warm, sweet pressure, a gentle understanding.

Except he *didn't* understand. Because he didn't know. She had to tell him. Tonight. But first she had to show him how much she loved him.

Her room was cool and quiet as he pulled back the quilt and laid her down. The scent of a bouquet of daffodils and freesias from Carissa's spring garden perfumed the air. Dappled moonlight shone through her lace curtains, dimming and brightening as clouds scurried across its face.

Enough light to see all of him as he stripped off his clothes without speaking. They both knew without words he was staying. He was beautiful—a perfectly proportioned *beautiful* man, in every way. In the moonlight his sharp, dark masculine lines and ridges melted into the soft sheen of silver where the moon coasted over his skin.

Lazy shadows curled and stretched as he approached the bed, placed his hands on either side of her waist and leaned over her.

'Melanie.' Her name drifted on the air like a balm, to soothe and to arouse as he slid warm palms beneath her jumper and up, sliding her arms out of the sleeves then over her head. Then her skirt, a slow rasp of zip, the rougher chafe of denim as he tugged it down over her hips.

'Purple?' he asked, his voice husky as his hands moved over her satin bra, cupping her breasts before unclasping it from behind, then gliding down her hips and slipping off her matching panties.

'Red.' The moon had leached all colour from the room, stripping it down to stark black and white and silver. The way he was stripping her, leaving nothing but the sheer simplicity and clarity of love.

In the dimness and slow-burning passion she ached to lose herself in Luke's loving and not think about tomorrow. 'Make love to me, Luke,' she whispered, wanting skin to skin, heart to heart, knowing everything had changed. Would change again too soon.

Tonight was different. For her, for him.

'You're not too tired?' he murmured.

'After seeing that little miracle tonight?' She shook her head against the pillow. 'I'm on a high—no, I'm not too tired.'

He took her raised hands, twining his fingers through hers and looked into her eyes. 'You are amazing. I've said it before, but now it's more. Much more.' He lifted their joined hands to his lips, pressed his open mouth to the pulse thrumming like a hummingbird's wings at her wrist.

Then he lay down and stretched out beside her, one hairy thigh against her hip. His heat, his need burned with an urgency tempered by a willingness to take it slow.

He whispered into her ear. 'First I'm going to kiss you until there's not a patch of skin I haven't tasted.'

She whimpered as he laved a path from ear to neck to breast. Did he know she trembled? Could he hear the way her heart thundered against his lips? Her own hands traced the hard slope of his shoulders and muscled upper arms, marvelled at the soft, sweet pull of his mouth on her nipple. Strength and tenderness.

He skimmed his lips over sensitised, goose-peppered flesh, his body abrading the sheets with a soughing sound as he moved down. Over thigh, knee, calf, ankle, toes, repeating his journey up the other leg.

He paused to pry her legs apart, looked up and met her eyes. What she saw in those depths was real and honest. Her heart swelled, her exposed flesh quivered as he lowered his head, lingered there with something close to reverence.

On a low groan he reared up on his knees and straddled her. With his attributes carved in moonlight and shadows he was that perfection she'd admired the first morning he'd come back into her life.

Then he lowered himself on top of her and her eyes drifted shut.

His mouth caressed hers, opened. Tongues met in a lazy tango of darkly rich tastes and textures, until kissing was no longer enough.

Spreading her thighs, she took him in, a slow, slippery glide of heat, a long satisfied sigh of completion. She arched her hips so he was deep, so deep it was as if he touched every part of her.

They'd never loved this way before, lingering over every touch, absorbing every sigh. Savouring every moment as if it were their last. Time slowed, stopped, became irrelevant.

'Look at me,' he murmured. 'I want to see those silver eyes with me all the way.'

She opened her eyes and his dark, passion-filled gaze melded with hers. He felt it too, she thought in wonder—the magic they made together.

Something stronger than magnetism drew them together, Luke thought. Her skin glowed beneath his hands. It wasn't moonlight; it was Melanie. Shining with her own inner radiance.

He watched her bloom anew as he buried himself deep in her dark velvet heat again, withdrew slowly, deliberately, until his entire body was throbbing with need.

But he bit back the groan that threatened to erupt from his chest, desperate to keep the mood easy. She needed a slow hand tonight after the hell-for-leather day she'd had.

Lazy gave him time to search for buried treasure he might have missed up till this point. He discovered the little sound she made when he rubbed circles behind her knees. When she began to squirm and sigh he used fingers and lips on her familiar trigger points until easy turned to urgent.

Until he steeped himself in her one last time, watching her eyes turn dark, then cloud with passion as he came and she flew apart beneath him.

Moments later, she nestled beside him as he watched the mottled moonlight play across the wall. 'Luke.' His name slurred slightly on her lips.

'No talk. Sleep now.'

'No. We *must* talk, I must tell you some—'

He looked down at her face, taut with fatigue, put a finger on her pursed mouth. 'Whatever you want to say can wait another day.'

'But—'

'No.'

Deliberately, he pulled the quilt up over his shoulder, closed his eyes. It was a brief minute or two before he heard her sleep-slow breathing. And not before time.

Dedicated, his Melanie, with a steely strength hiding a marshmallow core. And yet when he'd looked into her eyes in the kitchen earlier, he'd seen…vulnerability. Something was bothering her. Whatever it was, it would wait till morning. Whatever it was, he'd help her through it.

* * *

Luke woke to the sound of rain beating on the window and a warm body next to his. A sleeping body. He snuggled lower. Great weather for staying in bed and indulging in some morning glory, he thought, plumping his pillow so he could watch Melanie sleep.

Eyes closed, her hair in disarray on her pillow, a frown creasing her brow as if she saved patients even in dreams. Or fought demons, he thought with a frown of his own, remembering last night when she'd wanted to talk.

An arm shot up, hitting his nose and nearly knocking him out. Typical Mel. She never stayed still for long—he was amazed that he'd slept undisturbed all night. A testament to the long hours she'd put in yesterday, he guessed, his body tightening as the curve of Mel's bottom wriggled closer.

Down, boy. Right now she needed sleep more than she needed sex. But he couldn't resist easing the quilt down to see the gentle rise and fall of her breasts, the dark chocolate nipples jutting at him.

Okay. Option one. He could lie here and torture himself looking at the early morning light bring a tinge of colour to her creamy skin, feeling her warm breath on his shoulder. Or option two, he could go home and make a start on those boxes he'd taken to his apartment that he'd yet to sort. Come back in a few hours with breakfast.

Then take the afternoon showing Melanie that spending it in bed was… No. She'd be anxious to visit Carissa and little Robert Baxter Jamieson again. They could do that together, he thought, hauling his butt out of bed. He wanted to check on the little guy again himself to see if he'd changed any since last night.

It also got him thinking again as he pulled on yesterday's wrinkled and—he sniffed—vaguely odorous clothes. About kids and family. And Mel. And kids and family and Mel in the one sentence was a new step for him.

His gaze turned to Mel. As he watched she did a flip and

rolled onto her back. A hank of ebony hair obliterated half her face. Smiling, he crossed to the bed, smoothed it away.

And his heart swelled with…something. Something big. Something so huge it left no room for breath. He'd tried to ignore it; Melanie didn't want anything permanent—she'd made that quite clear.

But last night… She'd been different last night.

He stepped back quietly, shut her door behind him and let himself out into the rain. Maybe it was time to change her mind.

Back in his apartment he was on the floor and down to the last box. The junk of his life, he thought, glancing at old papers and magazines littering the space around him.

He pulled the last box nearer and took out a bundle of old correspondence. His forwarding address had been added in his father's handwriting, but it had missed the post by about five years.

He flipped through them. A dental reminder, a magazine subscription renewal, a letter. Business envelope—he turned it over—no sender info. He tore it open, slid out a single sheet of paper. Instantly recognised the handwriting.

He read the first line. Blinked, read it again.

'Luke, I'm pregnant…'

The lines blurred and he couldn't read any further. The paper slipped from his numb hands. His breath stalled in his chest; something was twisting his bowel into knots. His heart—he didn't know what to do with the jack-hammer pounding its way through his chest, the vice that was squeezing the life out of it. Nor the knowledge that—sweet heaven…

Mel had been pregnant.

With his child.

And somewhere in the part of his brain that was still functioning rationally a question: where was that child now?

CHAPTER SIXTEEN

THE noise pounded its way into her dreams, a relentless hammering that finally brought Melanie to a groggy awareness that someone was demanding to be let in. And that Luke was no longer lying beside her.

Pushing her hair out of her eyes, she sat up. Eleven forty-three! She grabbed her terry robe and struggled to her feet. 'I'm coming!' For God's sake.

Throwing the door open and squinting against the dark outline against the glare of daylight, she barely recognised Luke before he stalked inside. 'Oh…hi… Where have you been…?' She rubbed the heel of one hand across her eyes, pressed it to the dull throb in her temple. 'I'll have to get a key cut for you…'

Her voice trailed off as she finally looked at the man in front of her, fists curling and uncurling and smelling of rain. Muscles bunched on both sides of his unshaven jaw. His damp hair was furrowed, as if he'd run an exasperated hand through it.

But it was his eyes that brought her fully awake. Dark and roiling with a dozen different emotions.

Fear gripped her. 'What's wrong? It's not Carrie, is it?'

'What happened to our child?'

For a second she simply stared, stunned. Then her breath caught and her knees trembled while her pulse thundered sickly in her ears. How…? It didn't matter.

What mattered now was that he knew.

And he hadn't heard it from her.

'I…was going to…tell you last—' Old guilt coiled around

her heart, its venom dark and deadly. She tried to speak, to explain, but all that came out was the pitiful sound of her heart breaking. Again. Spots shimmered before her eyes and, unable to stand, she sank to the floor.

He stooped, gripping her upper arms. 'You were pregnant, Melanie—I found your letter amongst a pile of stuff Mum and Dad forgot to post.'

She closed her eyes as tears spilled down her cheeks.

'When I didn't answer your letter did you decide it was all too hard? That a child—*our* child—would've gotten in the way of your life?'

Horror and anger gave her strength. Struggling out of his arms, she pummelled his chest with all the fury and the pain and the anguish she'd borne alone for so long.

'How dare you think that? You weren't here.' She shoved him away. 'You have no idea *how* I felt, what it's like to be pregnant and alone. But, no, I did *not* have an abortion.'

A fraction of the tension eased from his face and something flickered in his eyes. He knew he was handling this all wrong. With a shake of her head, she staggered to her bedroom. She hugged her arms, remembering.

She felt Luke come up behind her but she didn't turn around. He ran his hands up and down her arms. 'You're shaking like a leaf. Sit down.' With an arm around her shoulders, he lowered her to the side of the bed and sat beside her, then let her go. Pulling away.

'Tell me,' he said, his voice oddly devoid of emotion.

Melanie closed her eyes. 'I had a miscarriage.'

'What happened?'

'I was lifting a tray of drinks and I slipped on some spilt champagne.'

Incredulity brought a slash of colour to his cheek-bones, turned his eyes dark. 'You kept working? Lifting heavy loads in your condition?'

'Yes,' she snapped. He wouldn't understand; he'd never understand what it was like to have to work to survive. 'I had no choice. I had to work.'

Luke's hand slipped into hers. That simple act also threatened to open a floodgate, so she didn't squeeze back. Instead she took a deep fortifying breath and stood up. They needed somewhere neutral, a place where they could talk without Adam interrupting them. 'Let's take a walk,' she said.

Without speaking they took Luke's car and drove two minutes to the local park. They walked for five minutes, making their way along a path overgrown with winter soursobs.

A chilly breeze chased away the rain but the old plane trees dripped moisture, cold drops spilling onto her face and down her neck and leaving droplets on Luke's hair and eyelashes. She wanted to reach out and connect with him but he didn't want that touch. He stood remote and grim—within touching distance but miles apart, shivering in nothing but a T-shirt, the hairs on his arms bristling with the cold.

'You didn't tell me. Five years ago…you should have done more.' Eyes as bleak and winter-cold as the day drilled into hers. 'And now we've been together weeks, and still you kept it to yourself.'

'I wanted to tell you, Luke. I was going to. I was waiting for—'

'Don't you know I'd have come back for you?'

The soul-destroyingly broken way he said that, almost as if he were laying his heart at her feet, ripped her to shreds. She shook her head. 'Why would I think that? You accepted a job interstate. You didn't include me in your plans.'

'No?' His lips flattened, his jaw clenched. 'You were in such a hurry to pack up and move on that night, I barely had time to finish dressing, let alone ask you if you'd take a chance and come with me.'

While she stood reeling at his words, he twisted away with a sharp exhalation, slapped a hand on the trunk of the tree they stood beneath. 'Where do we go from here?'

By the way he muttered it Melanie didn't think he expected a reply, and he didn't get one; she was fresh out of answers.

They drove back in silence but for the muted radio playing seventies hits and the click click of Luke's fingers tapping an agitated staccato on the steering wheel.

She half expected him to drop her off and continue on his way, but he accompanied her inside. To collect his jacket, she realised.

They stood in the room like two strangers. Her lip trembled as she watched him but she bit down on the inside until she tasted blood. She'd lost him.

Not that she'd ever had any claim to Luke Delaney, rich man's son or self-made millionaire.

He didn't even say goodbye. Just turned and walked out, closing the front door behind him. Closing the door on their relationship. Their *no-strings, casual* relationship.

Why should she have expected anything else?

Gripping Melanie's letter, Luke let himself into the old house with his key and headed for the bright glass-walled gazebo, a recent addition at the far end of the house where his parents spent their leisure hours.

The room's warmth from the pot-belly stove and the damp-earth smell from his mother's indoor plants greeted him as he shoved open the door.

He found his father asleep on his recliner, Sunday's news-paper on his chest, reading glasses halfway down his nose.

'Dad, where's Mum? I need to talk to both of you.'

His father opened his eyes. 'Hello, son. Your mother's gone to the city for some ladies' luncheon. Won't be back for hours.' He frowned. 'What's up? You look fit to kill.'

Near enough, Luke thought. 'This letter here—' he waved it in the air '—is from Melanie. She wrote it five years ago. It was in a bundle of mail you neglected to forward.'

His father adjusted his chair to its upright position, folded his newspaper, removed his glasses. 'I'm sorry, Luke. Was it something important?'

Tension snapped in Luke's jaw. 'I'd say so. She claims she tried getting in touch with me. I was wondering…did she ever phone here?'

Something flickered behind his old man's eyes. He pursed his lips, folded a hand over the other under his chin and looked out at the dripping garden beyond. Then he looked at Luke. 'Yes. She did.'

Luke's gut tightened as everything inside him shifted. 'You gave her the relevant address, then?' He managed—barely— to keep his voice civil. 'My phone number, my email address? You told her where I was?'

'I didn't want some itty-bitty waitress taking your attention away from your work—you were just starting to see success. I know she's made something of herself now, she might even be—'

'You didn't think to ask me what I thought?' Luke took a dangerous step closer. Dangerous because he didn't know if he could control the anger threatening to explode from his chest. He curled his fists against his sides. 'You didn't even want me taking up engineering geology. You wanted me here, to follow in your shadow.'

His father frowned. 'No, that's not true… I—'

'Do you know what you've done?' He crushed the paper and threw it on the floor in front of his father.

'You turned her away when she was pregnant.'

His father paled, but, stubborn as ever, predictable as ever, he said, 'Are you telling me she tried to trap you with that old line?'

'I'm telling you she had a miscarriage. A miscarriage that may have been prevented if I'd been there for her.' He drew a deep shuddering breath. 'I understand you may have over-looked the letter—you couldn't have known it was from her. But you cast her off like she was nobody.

'She was *somebody*, Dad. Somebody I cared about. Somebody I *still* care about. She was in trouble and she was pregnant. I got her that way, it was my responsibility.'

'Son, I—'

'Understand this, Dad.' He heard his own voice—dead calm, dead serious. 'Your actions may have cost you your only chance to be a grandfather.' He slammed an open palm on the door jamb on his way out.

Seeing Luke on her doorstep when he'd walked out only a couple of hours ago was a shock Melanie didn't need. Not when she was about to play auntie for the first time. She needed smooth and calm; no stress, and she wouldn't get it with Luke standing in her line of vision, saying, 'Melanie' in that 'we-need-to-talk' voice.

She didn't want to hear any more of that voice, which only last night had murmured he was going to kiss her all over. She didn't want to look at the gorgeous mouth that had done the job so thoroughly.

'I'm on my way to see Carissa and the baby,' she said. And since Carissa didn't deserve a red-eyed sister on her first day as a mum, she picked up her keys.

He wasn't deterred. 'What I have to say won't take long. I intend dropping past the hospital and seeing Carissa myself in a while.'

She didn't want to try to interpret his expression or why he seemed so anxious to talk. 'I want to see my sister on my own.' A bunch of other emotions she'd spent the past couple of hours trying to subdue were springing up again like grass fires. 'And the afternoon's slipping away…'

'Okay,' he said, stepping inside and closing the front door behind him. 'But first you *will* listen to what I have to say.'

He stood close enough for her to feel the heat from his body and smell the soap he liked to use. She had to force herself to look at him. Not the cold eyes from earlier, but intense emotions still lurked in the toffee-coloured irises.

'I asked you if you ever rang my parents, Melanie, and you said no.'

Her fingers tightened around the keys in her hand. Ah. This was about good old Dad. 'That's not true,' she said. She couldn't quite look him in the eye so opted for his chin. 'You didn't ask me that question, not in those words. You *suggested* I could've contacted them by phone.'

'To which you conveniently didn't reply.' Clearly agitated, he shifted his stance. 'Why didn't you tell me?' he demanded, his voice harsh with frustration.

'I didn't see the point since it doesn't make a difference now.'

Muscles clenched in his tight jaw. 'The hell it doesn't.'

'You were trying to reconnect with your parents. I didn't want to interfere with that. And it was a long time ago, we weren't serious…'

'Yeah, I know. *Single and loving it*—your words, not mine.' He shook his head. 'You just don't get it, do you? I don't want temporary any more. I want a family.'

Mel's heart swelled; she tried to squelch it. 'I want that too,' she whispered. And saw Luke's eyes widen, darken with a new awareness, then watched him mentally step back.

'I also want someone who can be honest with me at all times. Someone who won't keep secrets no matter how hard it is. You held back important information, first our pregnancy—yes, *ours,* Mel, make no mistake about that—then Dad's phone call.' He inhaled deeply through clenched teeth, then all the tension seemed to drain out of him, as if he'd lost some sort of battle. 'We're too different, Melanie.'

Leaning against the wall for support, she listened as his car purred into life and waited till the sound faded into the background traffic.

Before she could give in to the tears dammed behind her eyes, she opened the door and walked out into the rain. She walked for an hour, letting the moisture and cold soak into the pores of her face and chill her hands.

As she re-entered the apartment an echo of Luke's presence

still lingered, his subtle scent, the imprint of his mouth on hers, the deep timbre of his voice as he said those final words.

And he was right—they were too different. In so many ways. She loved him, but it wasn't enough. Not for Luke.

As her gaze swept the last place he'd stood when he'd told her, something on the floor caught her attention. It must have fallen out of Luke's jacket. She picked up the neatly folded paper.

A 'To Do' list.

Confirm: August 5th 6 o'clock
Organise tux.
Ring Eleanor
Arrange pick-up

Her keys slipped from her fingers as her blood drained to her boots. She'd thought her heart had broken, but this betrayal shattered her very soul.

In ten days' time he was attending a black-tie function with that old girlfriend with the fancy surname, and, if she wasn't mistaken, hiring a limo to pick her up.

On August 5th. Melanie's birthday.

Her fingers tightened on the damning evidence, her teeth ached as her jaw tightened, and anger—good, hard, cleansing anger-rose like a red wave.

And he'd talked about honesty.

She swiped her keys from the floor, grabbed her bag, crushed the paper inside and stalked to the door. She'd show him honesty! After she'd seen Carissa she was going to pay him a visit.

Carissa was sitting up in bed cuddling a sleeping young Robert when Melanie arrived. Ben watched over them protectively, last night's grin still firmly in place. A bright bunch of helium balloons was tied to the hospital crib beside the bed.

'Hi!' Melanie's heart squeezed tight at the beautiful image

of family. 'You're looking a darnn sight better than you did last night,' she said, bending down to give her sister a kiss. 'Don't leave it that late next time, you hear?' She dropped a kiss on Ben's cheek.

'Next time?' Carissa laughed softly.

'I was a nervous wreck and Luke…' Just saying his name filled her with a bitter-sweet longing. She had to fight to keep her smile in place.

Ben chuckled. 'Yeah, he looked a bit green when we left.'

'So did you, from what I remember, *Daddy*,' Carissa said, smiling down at her son. 'Isn't he beautiful?'

'Can I take a closer peek?' Melanie carefully loosened the flannelette rug and gazed at the tiny life. He looked back at her with unfocused eyes. A fist shot up then straight into his mouth and he began sucking noisily.

Melanie's own nipples tingled and the pull tugged at her womb. Tears welled in her eyes. 'He looks like Ben.'

His male ego stroked, Ben straightened and grinned. 'That's what Carissa said.'

'Honey, would you go get me…anything from the canteen?' Carissa asked sweetly. 'And take your time.'

Ben stood with a put-upon sigh. 'Okay, I know when I'm not wanted.'

As if she'd had a dozen children already Carissa gently removed the tiny fist and replaced it with the knuckle of her index finger. The moment Ben was out of earshot she wasted no time. 'Speaking of Luke…'

'Which we weren't,' Melanie pointed out, instantly feeling nauseous.

'He stopped by a few moments ago with the balloons. You just missed him. He seemed to be in a hurry.' Her gaze probed Melanie. 'He looked terrible.'

She didn't want to dump on Carissa today of all days but Carissa was relentless. She was also the only family Melanie had, and her best friend. 'It's over between us,' she said. 'And this time it's *really* over.'

Carissa frowned. 'Did he say that?'

'He didn't have to.' Melanie thought of the note in her bag. It kick-started her into action. 'I've got to be somewhere, sis.' She kissed baby Robert and Carissa. 'I'll see you again real soon.'

CHAPTER SEVENTEEN

MELANIE pulled up outside Luke's apartment. Again that sense of not belonging surged through her. And yet…his mother had come from humble beginnings.

Forget it. She reached for her bag, pulled out the note, read it again to remind her why she should 'forget it' before stuffing it in the pocket of her jeans.

Her skin prickled as she stepped out of the car, slammed the door, glared up at the apartment. Was he watching her from behind his sparkling panoramic windows?

But as she climbed the steps she realised it was his neighbour, Mrs Perfect, eyeing her from her balcony next door.

'Hello, can I help you?' she called.

Nosy woman. Melanie kept walking. 'No, thanks.'

'Luke's not home.'

Melanie frowned, pausing between steps. Did she keep an eye on his every move?

'He left around an hour ago,' the woman continued when Melanie didn't answer. 'I was out walking Poochie when the cab came and I heard him say he was going to the airport. So naturally I told him I'd keep an eye on the place for him.'

'Oh.' Melanie's anger fizzed and sputtered, doused by something closer to fear, and the colder knowledge that he'd probably left the country. 'Thanks,' she murmured, doing an about turn and retracing her steps.

Was his hasty departure an extreme reaction to the day's events that only the wealthy could afford to indulge in or had he planned to leave all along? No. He hadn't planned it, she was sure.

Except…he hadn't mentioned going to a function with Eleanor either.

Of course he wouldn't, just like those other times early on in their relationship when he'd gone to events without telling her. Their relationship wasn't that important to him; *she* wasn't that important to him.

Shock was sending debilitating shivers through her as she slid into her car and turned on the ignition with shaking fingers. They'd been lovers less than twelve hours ago. The closest they'd ever been. And not just lovers, they'd shared their thoughts and hearts as well as their bodies.

When she arrived home she saw the answering machine blinking. She pressed the button, her fingers clenching the phone when she heard Luke's voice.

'Mel, it's me.' Pause. 'Guess you're with Carissa.' Another pause as if he was composing what he wanted to say. 'Just letting you know I'm—'

She stared at the phone in her hand, then hurled it onto the couch. She'd forgotten to rewind the damn tape and missed the end of his message. But she already knew what he'd have said, she didn't need to hear it again.

Goodbye.

Melanie sat beside Adam as he drove south-west out of Sydney. Even if it was only five a.m., at least someone was prepared to lift her spirits and give her a happy birthday. The clear, cold morning sky was still dark and studded with stars, framing an old gibbous moon still high in the sky.

Adam had refused to talk about his surprise. He'd turned out to be more than a flatmate; he'd become a good friend. So he left his smelly socks on the couch, the toilet seat up. His wet towel in a pile on the side of the bath. He wasn't just a friend, he was an all-round good guy.

He was also a friend of Luke's.

The band around her chest tightened. She'd have to find new accommodation. Running into Luke wasn't an option if she wanted to start a new life. She'd heard Adam talking to him on the phone yesterday. From the gist of the conversation apparently Luke was back in town.

Which meant tonight he was going to rub shoulders with the rich and famous *and* the glamorous woman he'd been linked with five years ago. He might even rub more than shoulders with her.

For all she cared.

But she hunched into the vinyl seat, her nails digging moon shapes in her palms as images of Luke's body rubbing up against the blonde played out before her eyes.

She turned her mind to concentrating on the changing scenery as they reached the outskirts of the city. In the predawn not far from Burragorang State Conservation Area, she realised Adam was taking her hot air ballooning, something she'd always told him was on her list of things she wanted to do.

As soon as they arrived at the local airport Melanie was out of the car before Adam had even shut off the engine. Adrenaline pumped through her veins. 'Adam,' she breathed, cupping her hands around her mouth for warmth. 'You sure know how to make a girl's birthday.'

'It's a bit chilly.' Adam leaned into the back seat and held out a coat.

But not just any coat, she realised as soon as she took it. Caressed it. A three-quarter length white suede dream, soft as a marshmallow, with fur-trimmed hood.

Her eyes narrowed with suspicion. 'What the heck is this? You can't afford anything like this, and even if you could, I wouldn't take it.' They weren't *that* close.

He shrugged, sighed. 'I borrowed it. Don't ask questions, okay?'

'But it's new…' She squinted in the dimness. 'It's still got the price…'

But Adam jerked the tag off with a scowl and stuffed it in

his pocket before she got a proper look. 'Just wear the damn thing, will you?' he grumbled, shaking it out for her to put on. 'It's bloody cold up there.'

She lifted its smooth texture to her face, breathed in its expensive new scent. 'As long as it's not stolen property, I guess I can be persuaded.' She glanced sideways at him as she shrugged it on. 'It's not, is it?'

'No. Dammit. Come on.'

'You're in a fine mood for someone who claims to want to… wait a minute…' Her breath caught in her throat. 'This doesn't have anything to do with Luke… does it?'

'Yes, of course it does,' he groused. 'Didn't you two call it quits?'

Her stomach cramped. 'Can't you let me forget?'

'That's why we're here, isn't it? You're the one who brought the topic up.' He stopped, turned to her. 'Want to know what I think?' Catching her shoulders, he looked into her eyes long and hard till she squirmed. 'I think you're in love with him.'

'Huh!' Jerking away, she marched on towards the terminal, feeling the first sting of tears, determined not to let them fall. 'I didn't ask what you think. It's my birthday, let's just have a good time, shall we?'

Melanie listened with only half an ear as the group was briefed on the morning flight, but, despite her best intentions, her mind kept wandering back to Luke and this evening's function.

They were conveyed to the scheduled meeting point and her mind was temporarily distracted when she saw the first of the huge balloons being readied for flight, the whoosh and flare of burning propane gas, the balloon taking shape as it filled with air.

It took twenty minutes to inflate the two balloons, with some of the passengers helping, a magnificent sight in the predawn— a blue one with red and yellow squares, the other a glorious orange and green.

Crimson streaked the sky as the last stars faded and the balloon swayed slightly, ready to fly.

'That one's ours,' Adam said, grabbing her hand and heading towards the blue one.

'Good morning. I'm Jacob, your pilot for the next hour or so.' The tanned man with a sparkle in his eyes grinned as he helped Melanie aboard.

'Good morning.' Inside the wicker basket Melanie could see the bundles of cables, a two-way radio. The warmth and smell of the roaring burners.

'Ready for our aerial adventure?' he said, checking his equipment.

'You bet,' she shouted over the noise.

He grinned again—as if he was privy to some private joke—and said, 'Then you're in for the ride of your life.'

Better than the roller-coaster she and Luke— No. She wasn't going to spoil it. She turned her attention to the pilot. 'So, how does this thing work?'

Preoccupied, she hadn't noticed the other passengers had all headed to the other balloon until she turned to Adam behind her.

Except he wasn't behind her.

He was standing on the grass a few metres away with the glint of dawn's light in his eyes and a smile on his lips. He lifted his hand in salute. 'This is where I say good-bye...'

'What...?'

Her voice trailed off as a figure broke away from the other group and headed towards her balloon at a fast-track pace.

Her heart started pounding as the figure resolved into a big man wearing a long black coat buttoned to the neck. A too-familiar man.

'And good luck,' she heard Adam say.

But she was too busy staring at Luke and gathering her defences. All she could think of was how to make her legs work because they seemed to be glued to the bottom of the basket.

His strides devoured the space between them as the basket swayed, impatient to be airborne.

Luke's legs were vibrating like a drilling machine as he hurried across the dew-soaked grass. At the centre of his vision was the woman, her ebony hair at her shoulders lifting in the slight breeze. Suddenly it didn't matter that the sight of that flimsy contraption was enough to dry the spit in his mouth, that inside the tux beneath his coat he was sweating up a storm.

As he watched she lifted a hand and pressed it to her chest. That had to be good, right? It meant her heart was gallumping too.

But the vibes across the few metres separating them now weren't good—they blew through him like an Antarctic blizzard. Only the all-consuming need to reach her—just to touch her and make her listen to what burned in his heart—propelled him forward.

He passed Adam going the other way. 'Thanks, bud, I owe you,' he muttered.

Adam raised a hand. 'Go get her, mate.'

He'd expected the frown, the frosty-eyed panic in her grey eyes, though he'd hoped for something, *anything* from those thinned ashen lips that he could pin a hope on.

Her complexion matched the coat, he noted as he closed the remaining few metres. At least Adam had talked her into wearing it. She used it now, wrapping it tighter around her like a shield and backing as far away as she could in the confined space. He wouldn't put it past her to jump at the last moment.

Like a falling man scrabbling at the sides of a cave-in, he grabbed at the wicker and swung himself up beside her. 'Hi.' He cursed the breathlessness in his voice, the line of sweat snaking down his spine and into what must now be a very wrinkled dress shirt.

At that moment the balloon lifted off on a slow glide. He didn't look. His gaze was wholly focused on the woman in front of him, her face averted and turned to the dawn, its rosy hue painting her cheeks a soft peach.

'I take it the coat's yours as well,' she said without any word of greeting.

'No, it's yours.'

She stood ramrod straight and shook her head. 'It's too fancy to waste on me. I'd only get it dirty in my line of work. It suits someone who'd wear it the way it's supposed to be worn. In style.' Her voice had a barb that speared through his chest as she finally pinned that frostbite gaze on him.

Melanie looked into his mesmerising eyes, eyes that seemed to draw her inside his skin, as if she were part of him, and was almost tempted to take what they'd always had—fun times, surprises, sensational sex.

But when you stripped that away, what was left?

'I know these past weeks haven't been easy but we can get through this, Mel.'

She shook her head slowly. *And when we come out the other side, what then?*

'I want you,' he said, grabbing her hands before she could pull away. 'Your spontaneity, your energy, your colour. You're full of surprises. I never know what's going to happen next.'

She saw the depth of passion in his eyes, felt it in the hard grip of his hands, heard it in his words. But her heart throbbed as if he'd pummelled it with that passion.

He wanted her.

Yes, he wanted her in his bed but he didn't want her accompanying him to functions. Good enough for a private show, but a liability in public.

Well, it wasn't enough—she had some pride left.

'It won't work for us, Luke,' she said, pulling away so he wouldn't feel the tremor in her hands, so she didn't feel the ache in her chest so acutely. She turned her gaze skyward, at the balloon filling her vision. 'I don't know whether it was five years ago or five weeks, but somewhere along the line I fell in love with you. Against all the rules, I know, and it hurts too damn much.'

'Mel—'

He reached for her but she threw up a hand. 'Don't. Touch. Me. Please.'

'We can make it work,' he said quietly.

'Not without honesty.' Defeated, she looked out across the green belt of forest in the distance. 'You said so yourself.'

'I was so wrong that afternoon. I realise now that you did everything you could to let me know, to give me a chance to be part of your life. That you didn't want to hurt me by telling me the truth about the phone call.'

She gritted her teeth and braced herself. 'And you, Luke? Can you say you've been honest with me?'

'I'm not sure I follow.'

'No?' She swung to face him. 'What about the woman you're escorting tonight? Your six o'clock dinner date? Eleanor,' she elaborated when he continued to stare at her, slack-jawed and speechless as the balloon continued to rise. 'I found your list, Luke. Is it one of your father's functions?'

'*Eleanor?*' Something seemed to crystallise in the depths of his eyes. And was that tiny lift at the corner of his mouth the beginnings of a smile?

Because he was anticipating the evening ahead?

Inside her chest anguish and anger waged a vicious war, but she didn't look away from him. Oh, no. She needed to hear the truth from those lips, to read it in his eyes. Then perhaps she could move on. He might think he had her cornered but he was the one trapped now. Trapped by his own written words.

'The woman I'm escorting tonight?' he said finally. 'Oh, she's a stunner all right and she can mix it with the best of them. Even has my dad hooked. And I'm hoping it will be an engagement celebration.'

The last sentence, spoken in that husky voice with something close to reverence, slid through her like a knife. Everything alive inside her—every dream, every desire, every hope— drained away leaving an empty, aching hollow.

She could only stand mute and watch as he unbuttoned his

coat, shrugged it off and pulled out something from the inside pocket of his tux— His *tux?*

At that moment the first rays of the sun slid over the horizon, turning his tanned skin golden, glinting in his eyes.

'She's an intelligent woman too, the woman I love—at least I'd thought so until now.' He glanced down at whatever he held, then searched Melanie's gaze.

The woman he loves?

She didn't move. Couldn't. Her pulse hammered through every part of her body. Her mind was a blur. Six o'clock; six a.m.? Was she brave enough, strong enough, to entertain the thought that she'd got it all wrong?

When she remained rigid, he shook his head. 'This isn't going as planned—but with you, I suppose I should've expected that.' His lips curved just a little. 'Stop trying to analyse, Melanie, and listen with your heart.'

'But Eleanor… You were going to pick—'

He sighed, but his eyes were warm, crinkling at the corners as his smile widened. 'Your heart, Mel.'

Stepping closer, he touched the space between her breasts. Her heart pounded against his hand, whispered in her mind: *The woman he loves.*

'I don't understand.' Her voice trembled out.

'The only thing you need to understand is that I love you. *You*, Melanie Sawyer. Yes, we're different. And that's what I love about us. We complement each other, that yin and yang thing.

'As for the rest…Eleanor's married to the owner of one of the most exclusive jewellers in Sydney. "Ring. Eleanor"' he repeated, spacing the two words. 'That damn list—not a verb, Mel. "Ring" as in the circle of promise you give the woman you want to spend the rest of your life with.'

Melanie's breath caught. *The* ring…? The rest of her life?

He held it up so the sun sparked fire on gold, flashed in the stones, then reached for her hand. 'I hope you like amethyst and yellow diamonds. Marry me, Melanie.'

The words glittered in the air like the precious stones he was offering her. All the words she'd never thought she'd hear from Luke. 'You're serious.' Her heart soared with the balloon, her knees trembled as she looked into those familiar toffee eyes and saw the depth of his words mirrored there.

'Whoa.' As she sagged towards him Luke spread his legs a little, tucking her close against him with a breathless laugh that caught in her hair as he pressed firm lips to her temple. 'Damn right, I'm serious.'

Happiness was breaking over her like the warmth of the sunrise, but, 'What about your career, your father...?'

'I'm changing careers. I've had enough of overseas—the people who matter live here. I've just spent the past week sorting things out, inducting new staff to take over for me. I'm going into the hotel business with Ben since I hope we're going to be brothers-in-law. And you have your own career for as long as you want.

'As for Dad...' He leaned back and looked her straight in the eye. 'You changed his mind, honey. With your strength and loyalty and, yes, *honesty*. You didn't denounce him to me because you didn't want to put me in an awkward situation and he damn well knows it. He's keeping the champagne cold for us.

'So...' He lifted her hand in his hard-palmed one and rubbed a thumb over her knuckles. 'Will you share the rest of your amazing event-filled adrenaline-charged life with me?'

Her heart swelled, her throat clogged as her eyes filled with moisture. 'Yes,' she breathed.

She watched as he slid the ring onto her finger. Sighed as he brushed his lips over hers. She heard the low groan in his throat as she opened her mouth and mated her tongue to his. Her whole body quickened as he pulled her closer, his hands cupping her cheeks. She was soaring...

'Congratulations,' a cheery voice said, breaking into the moment and reminding Melanie of another reason why she was experiencing that lighter-than-air feeling.

She smiled at Jacob over her shoulder. 'Thank you.'

'Now you two have got that sorted,' he said, nodding to the sunrise, 'you might want to enjoy what's left of the flight and admire the view while we're up here.'

'Thanks, Jacob.' Luke grinned, his hands in Melanie's hair, finally dragging his gaze away from her to look about him. 'For a while there I thought we might have to stay up here for ever... And it's not as bad as I'd feared.'

'It's glorious,' Melanie said, hugging Luke's arm. 'Look, the other balloon.' They watched the balloon drifting like a giant orange some distance away. To the west she could see the smoky blue haze that gave the Blue Mountains their name. To the east, Sydney's skyline gleamed in early morning sun. She turned to Luke. 'You always swore no one would ever get you up in one of these.'

'No one but you.' He brought her left hand to his lips and kissed her newly ringed finger. 'I'd expected to be tossed like the wind, but it's so calm.'

Melanie grinned at the pilot. 'Because we're flying with the currents, right, Jacob?'

'Yes,' he replied. 'All smooth sailing.'

And all too soon they were on the ground again, and making their way to where a champagne breakfast had been set out on the lawn on the grounds of a stately old home. Plates of food and sparkling crystal flutes adorned snowy white tablecloths. Melanie's mouth watered at the aroma of bacon and hot coffee wafting their way.

In the distance she could see Luke's parents and Adam, Ben holding a blue-capped bundle in one arm and Carissa hanging on the other. Adam saw them first, then they all turned. At Luke's thumbs-up, they lifted their champagne glasses. Melanie's steps faltered as she saw Colin break away from the group and head towards them.

Luke's hand tightened on hers. 'He wants a moment with you, Melanie. Give him a chance to apologise.' Then he squeezed, let go and walked towards the others.

Which left her alone with the man who'd given her nothing but grief. In the sun's glare he looked older, his skin lacked its normal healthy glow, the lines around his mouth showed stress or pain. Perhaps he wasn't well, as he'd claimed, and she made a mental note to make sure he checked himself in to a doctor.

She could never forget what he'd done, but for Luke's sake she could try to forgive. She stopped a few feet away. 'Hello, Colin.'

'Melanie.' He nodded. 'Congratulations.'

'Thank you.'

His mouth worked a moment before he spoke again. 'I'm sorry. I was wrong.' He shook his head. 'Here I am, a man who's never been lost for words, and I can't think of a damn thing to say. To make it right between us…'

'You just did,' Melanie said, and took that first step towards her future father-in-law. She touched his arm lightly, caught the unfamiliar glint of her ring as she did. It brought a rush of emotion to her throat. She was going to be a part of Luke's family. 'We can talk another time. Shall we join the others?'

They walked together in silence. Maybe one day soon, she thought, they could converse like family.

As they approached Carissa broke away from the group and rushed into Melanie's arms. 'Oh, Mel, it's been so hard keeping the secret for a whole twenty-four hours,' she said as they headed towards the rest of the group.

Luke held out a single glass of bubbly. 'To share,' he told her and raised it to her lips. 'Happy birthday.'

Eyes on his, she took a sip, then turned the glass so his lips touched the same spot and returned the favour. 'It's one birthday I'll never forget.'

Hours later, Melanie lounged back beside Luke in his spa, enjoying the soothing balm of the water, the charcoal aroma from their barbecue tea. The lazy aftermath of hot and strenuous sex.

Wisps of steam curled off the surface as he lifted the bottle of champagne. 'Another?'

'Please.' She held out her glass.

'I've been thinking,' he said, topping up his own. 'I know Mum would love to plan our wedding—what do you think? You do want a wedding, don't you, Mel?'

'Hmm. I have to warn you that what I'd like might be a little less-than-traditional for your parents' tastes.'

'Ah.' He nodded. 'I already warned her. She said whatever you wanted was fine by her. Guess she doesn't know you as well as me.'

'Don't worry, it won't be anything too outrageous.'

'I've a feeling we'll be seeing a lot of them,' he warned gently.

'And wait till the grandchildren come...' She said it without thought, without sadness, but Melanie's skin prickled, and the air stirred as if someone had brushed by her.

Had Luke felt it too? Silent, he stared up at the night sky and for a few moments the only sound was the churning of the water jets.

In the dimness, he turned to her, his soul-deep eyes glittering like black jewels. 'We'll make more babies, Mel, if that's what you want.'

'Oh, I do.' She brushed at the tears welling in her eyes.

'Well, then...' His serious eyes turned mischievous and he grinned, tugging her hand beneath the water to where she discovered he was already up for the task again.

'How soon?'

'How soon?' Water sluiced off his body as he stood and picked up the nearby box of condoms. Tossed it neatly onto the still-smouldering barbecue. 'No need to wait for the big day. We'll start right now.'

EPILOGUE

Nine months later

THE theatre was austere white with green linoleum. His face was probably the same shade, Luke thought as he clutched Melanie's hand. Lights made the room as bright as day. Behind the green drape over Mel's body the doctor was preparing for a Caesarean delivery.

'Ready, Melanie?' the doctor said.

'Yes.' Her voice was calm, her smile almost serene. Only the tiniest hint of nerves flickered in her grey eyes.

Luke was glad of the mask hiding his expression. How could she be so composed when his gut was churning like an excavation drill and his pulse was running like a piston?

'Making the incision now.'

Luke knew she couldn't feel it. But he could. His blood drained to his feet and he gripped Mel's hand tighter as nursing staff went about their business as if this was any other day.

This wasn't any other day. In a few moments he'd be a father. He didn't know if he was ready to be a father yet. Too late. *Shouldn't have thrown away those condoms so soon,* an inner voice said.

'Luke. Honey? You have the camera ready?'

'Right here.' Somewhere.

'Would you like to watch the birth, Mr Delaney?' someone said, looking at him over her mask.

He cringed inwardly. 'No. Thank you. I'm fine, right here. My wife needs me…right here.'

Melanie smiled at him and squeezed his hand, but his clever wife could see right through him.

He needed her, not the other way round. She was strong and sexy and smart. She was colour and movement and life. She was the most beautiful woman he'd ever seen, even now, swathed in hospital linen.

Especially now.

He made a solemn vow to himself and Melanie as he sat on that chair stroking her hand, that whatever happened he'd be there for her and their children. They'd be there for each other.

Okay, he had a lot to learn about this new role and he was bound to make mistakes, just as his father had.

'A boy.' A voice intruded on his thoughts.

His heart almost leapt out of his chest. 'A son.'

'And a daughter. Congratulations, you two. A perfect pair of twins.'

'I love you so much, Mel,' he whispered, touching his lips to hers—gently, afraid of hurting her. She seemed so fragile lying on the operating table. 'Thank you.'

'Who's going to hold who?' another voice demanded.

He looked up through blurred eyes to see a nurse with two tiny bundles. 'It doesn't matter.'

The nurse laid one wrapped infant in his arms. 'This is—' he loosened the sheet '—Eliza—after her grandmother. Gorgeous, just like her mum.' He carefully laid her on Melanie's chest.

'So you must be…yep, you're definitely Cameron.' His tiny son opened his eyes and waved both fists at him. 'Going to be a handful, just like your cousin Robbie.'

'I think Eliza's going to take after me,' Melanie told Luke, gazing at her two-day-old daughter through the Perspex sides of the crib.

Luke paced the floor with a fussy Cameron. 'In that case we'll have to lock her up when she's sixteen.'

'I know I said I wanted to go back to work in a couple of years, but I think my nursing days are on hold indefinitely. I want to put my energy into raising these kids…and any others that come along.'

'Talking about more already?'

She looked at her family and her heart filled with love. 'Oh, yeah. But the Rainbow Road still needs me,' she said. 'I want to use any spare time to make it bigger and better. It's always been a passion of mine…'

A snuffle followed by a lusty wail signalled Cameron had had enough of being joggled by his father and was ready for sustenance.

'Now you and I have the funds to make that a reality,' she continued, unbuttoning her nightgown, already feeling the prickling sensation in her nipples that her babies' cries brought on.

No sooner had she got him settled and sucking, than Eliza, not to be outdone, joined in from her crib.

'Hey, darling, you feeling left out? Come to Daddy,' Luke crooned, picking her up, cradling her as if she were the most precious china.

'Okay, sweetie, there's enough for you too,' Mel said.

With Luke's help she adjusted both infants to feed at the same time. 'A-h-h. Quiet.' But she smiled as she said it.

Luke sat on the edge of the bed, lifted a strand of Mel's hair away from her face, smoothed his fingers over her lips. 'Now *I'm* feeling left out.'

A long, lingering, stubble-jawed kiss later, Melanie looked up at Luke. 'You need some sleep too, honey. And a shave might help.'

He looked tired and dishevelled. And damn irresistibly sexy…

Hmm. Juggling sex around feeds was going to take some manoeuvring. At the moment sex seemed as remote as the moon, but loving—the kind of loving that made no demands, the kind she saw in Luke's eyes right now—was there for keeps.

She'd thought nursing was busy, but with a husband and twins...

As if he read her mind he smiled. 'Life's about to get a lot more hectic.'

She lifted her face for one more prickly kiss. 'I wouldn't have it any other way.'

* * * * *